# THE BRIDPORT PRIZE

## POETRY AND SHORT STORIES

JUDGES

Martin Booth • Short stories
Paul Hyland • Poetry

Sansom & Company

First published in 1997 by
SANSOM & COMPANY
81g, Pembroke Road, Bristol BS8 3EA
for BRIDPORT ARTS CENTRE,
South Street, Bridport, Dorset



ISBN 1 900178 41 9

British Cataloguing-in-Publication Data.
A catalogue record for this book is available from the British Library.



Typeset by Mayhew Typesetting, Rhayader, Powys and printed by Hobbs the Printers, Totton, Hampshire.

# Contents

MARTIN BOOTH

# Story Report

Judging a prestigious short story competition such as this starts off as a monumental chore and winds up as a delight to be savoured.

The first phase is being sent, in box after cardboard box, all the submissions – over 3500 of them this year – every one of which I've read with one immediate criterion to be met: the story has had to grab me from the start. This is not narrow- or bloody-mindedness on my part. A short story has to be succinct, punchy, direct, capture you instantly: it is to literature what a bowl of Iron Buddha tea is to a Szechuan meal. It has to set the taste buds alight at once or it will fail to deliver the fine flavours to come.

The bulk sorted, the next phase is reading through, on this occasion, 451 stories. These get read from start to finish again, but quickly. They are the wine cellar of the competition. I have a go at each bottle to decide the best vintages. It is tedious, back-aching, eye-straining and often brain-numbing work for the outstanding ones have to be sifted from a lot of at least above average tales. Fine weather, a bottle of chilled Muscadet and a large garden table help: fortunately, I had all three this year.

From 451, I wound up with 111 stories I thought were good enough to take through to phase 3. The plots were at the very least adequate, the titles usually good, the typing neat, the manuscripts (well, mostly) grammatically sound. At this stage, in a prestigious competitive contest like this, professionalism is a distinct factor. Poor spelling, lay-out, punctuation and printing tell: several stories reached this far but died because the printer ribbon had been so faint as to make them unreadable save in direct sunlight. The century or so were then whittled down to a long list of 55.

At this point, life gets tough for the competitor and enjoyable for me for now, in the quiet of my study, the stories have to convince me, entertain me, educate or enlighten me, transport me to their worlds. In short, they have to really start working. Now is the time the real short story writers appear – the sheep are long since sorted from the goats: now I'm looking for the prize rams and unique Dollys. These are people who have borne several seminal points in mind. They have to be aware of structure, of originality, of the power of succinct narrative, of accurate dialogue, of the strength of character (and the spare construction of it in short fiction) and, above all else, they have to be conscious of what I like. A judge is, after all, someone they must not just reach through to and impress, but they must please him as well. A cook can make a fabulous tuna mousse but I can't eat tuna. . . So it is with short stories: I have my tastes and these are no secret. They can be discovered by an artful competitor with a quick trip to the library, a glance at my own books, my interests, my literary foibles.

Now the last phase kicks in. I read the long list, write notes on the covers, star the better ones and start to have fun myself. I ride off into the plains of others' imaginations, admire their language, wallow in their stories and not infrequently kick myself for not thinking of such a good idea. I am no longer a judge but a fellow writer in the company of peers.

The last prize winners are the hardest. I mull and procrastinate and argue with myself and show the stories to my wife, son and daughter. They are not judges, just sounding-boards. In the end, the decision is mine.

And now I have made it. As I send off the list of prize-winners to the organizer – they are just numbers to me still – I wonder about whose career I might be jump-starting, who will get a letter a fortnight hence saying *Dear X, I am very pleased to inform you. . .* And I remember the only literary prize I ever won, a Gregory Award in 1970 (I think) presented to me by Philip Larkin, who was one of my literary gods.

The last time I judged the Bridport Prize was five years ago. The first prize-winner went on to become a published novelist.

Is this where **Philip Raines** of Glasgow is heading? His story has won first prize. *Fado* is a bizarre, curious, captivating, unputdownable but hard-to-come-to-terms-with tale set in the Balkans (in Constanza in Romania, perhaps?). I found it hauntingly strange, puzzling and thoroughly original: it gave me several nights of macabre dreams. What was more, I suspected it was submitted by a Romanian or somesuch, for it is so accurate: that is some praise. Perhaps Mr. Raines is a diplomat, an aid worker, an avid tourist. Or he has one hell of an imagination and a distinct flair for research. Mind you, second prize winner, **Alan Tuppen** from London, could also readily travel on to greater things. His story, *Summer Lightning,* set in modern-day Malaysia, is poignant and touching but it is not just this that caught me. The dialogue is superbly studied and realistic, the atmosphere magically recaptured, the characters sparse but deep and genuine: it reminded me, and not just because of its setting, of a latter-day Somerset Maugham. Has he been to Malaysia? I suspect so. . . Third prize goes to **Suhayl Saadi** in Paisley who submitted a number of stories, only one of which was not (in my opinion) up to the long list. Here's another writer who could also develop into a notable published writer. *Rabia* is a fantasy love story with a poetic sadness to it which has been superbly handled. To them congratulations! Keep at it for you have what it takes.

Having said that **Tom Bryan**, **Anne Lewis**, **John Gohorry** and **George Burns** also have, I believe, what it takes. It is just that, on this occasion, for various reasons, they didn't quite compete with the top runners, didn't quite pull it off, send in their best work, or whatever. They all receive supplementary prizes which, I hope, will act as encouragement.

Below them come the three runners-up **Amanda Metcalfe**, **Kimio Yoshimura** (who lives in Japan) and **Penny Simpson**. They, too, have promise – they must have for they may be the bottom three but are still in the top one per cent of the year's submissions.

Every year I have judged this competition – and this is the third time in 15 years – I have observed trends. After cutting out stories about rabbits (*Watership Down* revisited), with main characters called Fenella Edwina Benbow-Crosse or opening lines that read, '*Don't look now chums, but I think we're coming under fire!*', specific directions appear. This year, there were a number of *Trainspotting*-type stories, most of them derivative (save George Burns' which was original) and not a few spawned by *The X-Files*. Amanda Metcalfe's story was perhaps one of these. Love stories are common, often commonplace and tedious: if romantic stories are your forte, at least be original. Stories with foreign climes in them are becoming increasingly common and that's a Good Thing. Nothing is worse than parochialism in anything. John Gohorry's story is about a Chinese dissident. What is also very good is the slight but gradual increase in overseas competitors entering: amongst the prize winners, 4 come from Scotland, 3 from England (but one of those is from Carlisle, which is almost Scotland), 2 from Wales and one from Japan. I'm not implying Scotland or Wales are overseas – but what's creatively going on in these 'provinces' of New Britain?

Overall, this was a good year, I feel. The winners are original and the long long list was the longest I've ever had in such a competition, which suggests that standards are rising. This might partly be due to entries being far more easily read, word processed, spell- and grammar-checked and, finally, well printed. Yet, that said, no word processor has devised a good story. Yet. No doubt, that day will come and, when it does, I'll not be the judge – my computer will be – and I shall be sidelined, miserable and unwanted, like the 747-400 pilot who is only needed when something goes wrong with his in-flight computer systems. I hope the day will never come. In truth, I think it won't but it wouldn't surprise me to discover this was the subject of a short story next year. . .

**Martin Booth**

*Biographical Note:* Martin Booth is a novelist, non-fiction author and children's writer: he also writes for both television (documentaries) and the cinema. His latest novel is *Adrift in the Ocean of Mercy*, whilst his latest non-fiction book is a literary biography, *The Doctor, The Detective & Arthur Conan Doyle.* His children's novel, *War Dog,* was a runner-up for the 1997 Children's Book of the Year Award. He is currently writing a new history of the Triads, the Chinese international criminal fraternity and working upon the first full biography of Aleister Crowley as well as a biography of Sir Richard Burton.

PAUL HYLAND

# Poetry Report

This is how it is for a judge. Hefty boxes are dumped on the floor. Peggy Chapman-Andrews, whom we must thank for initiating and sustaining this competition, and I have carried them from her car to my kitchen. The thousands of papers in the boxes are self-proclaimed poems, anonymous ones, distinguished only by numbers and by style of presentation: everything from scraps of scrawl torn out of notebooks to sumptuously word-processed and decorated documents on coloured paper.

When I open the boxes what am I looking for? I am looking for poems. I am waiting for the hairs on my nape to rise, for my mouth to dry a little, for my stomach to lurch, for my mind and my heart (if I could discriminate so neatly between thought and feeling) to say, Yes. I am looking for poems I like, and for poems I admire. If I am lucky I may find some that I both love and respect.

Soon, as I read, I begin to wish that many of the writers had respected even the elementary rules, that they had taken the trouble to read some twentieth-century poetry, perhaps even risked reading fine poems that are being written now. They could also have read a book or two about writing: for example, Michael Baldwin's *The Way to Write Poetry* (Elm Tree Books), Matthew Sweeney and John Hartley Williams's *Writing Poetry* (Teach Yourself Books), Peter Sansom's *Writing Poems* (Bloodaxe Poetry Handbooks 2), or, if they needed to demythologise the whole business and orientate themselves in the poetry world, my own *Getting Into Poetry* (Bloodaxe Poetry Handbooks 1). Some serious, enjoyable reading would have prevented many of the errors of judgement I'm staring at.

Fleur Adcock's *The Prize-Winning Poem* ends with the lines:

What is required is simply the masterpiece we'd all write if we could.
There's only one prescription for it: it's got to be good.

I'm looking for poems I think are good: a poem for which the poet has found the language, its own voice; a poem with good spelling and punctuation; a poem which hasn't already been written many times and much better; a poem which has a confident and properly ambitious sense of itself, without being embarrassingly self-conscious or pretentious; a poem whose form artfully harnesses and channels its raw power but does not cramp and confine it like an ill-made corset or an inescapable cage. A poem which needed to be written; a poem which sings; a poem that is a poem.

I had hoped to find one poem that rose above the rest and demanded first prize. I read and re-read my long shortlist, left them to rest in my head and returned to them. Again and again. In the end I found two and divided first and second prizes between them. I phoned all the winning numbers through and got the authors' names.

**Sheenagh Pugh's** *Crossing the Bridge* builds an airy structure, triplets made of just the right words, and carries us over on a narrative apparently so simple, though commenting upon itself, that its physicality and metaphysicality are utterly persuasive, truly moving, perfectly still. Three lives are changed.

**John Gurney's** *The Neutral Angel* finds the voice to tell a grimmer story in four well-made rhyming stanzas of (almost consistent) decasyllabics. The strict form contains the poem's awful passion, empowering rather than taming it. Every phrase – such as 'Out of reach' and 'spends the hours' in the third stanza – is just and telling. Does '"It's for the Minister!"' comfort, or collaborate in paranoia? Decide for yourself and see how the poem earns its brilliant, chilling conclusion.

In *The Sudden Shower* **Jonathan Davidson** deliberately begins with a cliché – 'Time tells' – but re-invigorates it. The poem's details are so precise, the language so fresh, that a whole childhood world and whole person(s) are economically evoked. They enlarge in the mind and touch us with sensuous insight into life and art.

**Amanda Dalton's** *How to Disappear* is a funny, ironic prescription that is seriously playful – a childish rite for desperate (or realistic?) adults. It finds its own rhythm and does good things with sounds and line-endings. It is not just about, for example, self-effacement, inferiority complex or anorexia. Read it and see how big it is. How it vanishes.

**John Godfrey** gave his winning poem the unarresting but apt title *Time and Place.* Many, many entries had variations on that title; most were bland or sentimental exercises in nostalgia. This one, in scrupulous near-rhyming quatrains, brings a present-day visitor, with her restrained American voice, to war-time Suffolk where a young GI meets his girl. Subtly it realises the sense of *déjà vu*, and culminates in delightful intimacy; a deft and powerful final image which does the job (apparently) effortlessly.

**Joan Wiles's** *Stephanotis* has a black voice which tells an old story (shades of Billie Holliday and many more) with power and modulated anger. In *Cornerstone* **Jane Beeson** finds strong and treacherous moorland images for the sexual politics that concern her. I might have concluded that *The Sudden Shower* and *Time and Place* were written by women, though I suspected the opposite. *Bukovina* I clearly heard in a man's voice; **Alison Spritzler-Rose** had surprised me by creating a quirky and convincing world of loss and sourness, illuminated by some dazzling lines. **William Palmer** enjoys himself in *The Good Ship Empire* and indulges us with an anarchic parody of colonialism in which domestic and exotic images are shaken and stirred.

*Honey* by **Trevor McMahon** gives us a magical image of masculine would-be control and female power. **Ciarán Ruby's** spare poem, *The Carrickatine Disaster. . .*, tells its words like beads and ends with the only image that might transcend irresolveable grief. *The Faust Family* takes many risks. If they had all come off I would have given **Clare MacDonald Shaw** a bigger prize. Its moments of brilliance deserve far more than faint praise. It does earn its necessary ending. **Len Krisak** offered a good number of poems, as did several other entrants. In *Gliding* he achieves a strenuousness which does not preen itself but makes, out of desperate matter, a fine sonnet.

**Angela Dove's** *The Corset* is rich, strange and recognizable. The play of pain and rite against surreal religiosity appealed and let me take it forward in my own head. *Washing and Astronomy* by **Judith Lal** was one of many poems about comets. I wanted to edit it, but the last four lines are wonderful. The subject of **Alex Smith's** *The Madness of my Sister* could have profited from Amanda Dalton's instructions. I read many poems of pathological self-loathing in the course of judging this competition, of which many were sickeningly exploitative or simply out of control. This one is poised, Manichaean, credibly disturbing.

I enjoyed living with my shortlist. Thank you. Many poems nearly made it. I felt sorry for superb lines stranded in indifferent poems and for good poems flawed by one discordant note. Like every other judge, I urge all entrants to read poems old and new. Enjoy writing your own and testing your limits. Be arrogant enough to take on your subjects, and humble in the face of them. Find the language and form that fits each piece of work. Write poems that discover themselves and end, not with some sort of self-satisfied punch-line that slams shut, but with lines which open a door and lead the reader out into the world a little larger for the experience.

**Paul Hyland**

*Biographical Note*: Paul Hyland has recently returned to live in Dorset. His last book, *Backwards Out of the Big World* (HarperCollins 1996, Flamingo 1997), was a book of the year in both the *Guardian* and the *Sunday Times*. His latest collection of poetry is *Kicking Sawdust* (Bloodaxe 1995). His *Getting into Poetry* (Bloodaxe, revised edition 1996) is universally acknowledged as, to quote Suzi Feay in *Time Out*, 'essential reading. . . *the* guide to the contemporary poetry scene'.

PHILIP RAINES

# Fado

*"If you want to be my man and always have me by your side."* Bela recites while playing soccer with the slum orfani, "*Well, don't speak to me of* fado. *Tell me about love.*"

Bela has been saying this over and over for the last hour of our hunt, mixing up the words hopelessly. I cannot explain how strange it is to hear him speak the lines of that tender song as we pause and look down on the city. Ever since my father first played *Fado's Sentence* to me, I have lived with the frail Elena Csonga version of the song, and now here is huge Bela, trampling through the words like a child loose in a garden. He misquotes them so brightly and innocently that it is almost impossible to remember how they dripped with the weariness and delicate heartsick of the ageing Csonga's voice. But it is churlish of me to complain. After all, it was at my urging that Bela is now learning how to read by studying the lyric sheets of my old cassette boxes.

This it also Bela's simple way of expressing the joy of the chase. For most of the evening, the two of us have pursued our prey, following it from the sugar port where I first caught its trail, through the Downtown where it skulked behind the tourist casinos, feeding on dinner-dance scraps, scampering through the Piata Presei Libere tunnel under the bay, across the ring boulevard, and finally dodging up the southern slopes. Since then we have been picking our way among the *saracacios* shanties, listening through the curdle of arguments, moans and radio pop for the distinctive trace of the quarry, certain that it must be somewhere near. I have tried asking families lying outside their one-room shacks in deference to the humid night, but none admit to seeing the dog.

"The *domnule* is looking for the *caine*?" A fat woman, her crippled leg supported by a truck tyre, replies with a shrug. "Who is not looking for the *caine*?"

"God favour your leg," I dismiss her and go back to Bela, who is showing the group of boys pictures of the national team in his copy of *Gazeta Sporturilor.*

"Did you find the dog?" Bela asks, excited, but when I shake my head, he is so disappointed I have to pat his shoulder. "But you *always* find the dog, Emil."

"*Domnule,* have you lost your dog?" one of the small boys asks. "I will find it for you!"

"And how would you know which is my dog, little *sire*?"

The boy whistles part of the dog's song, demonstrating an uncanny hearing that must surely lead to a future as a rag-ear. "In exchange, *domnule,*" he says to me and points at the sports paper.

"That would be fine, *sire,* were it my paper to offer. But it is not. It is my friend's."

"My friends?" Bela always looks surprised when someone shows respect for his things. "Oh, Emil, he can have the pictures, but I want to keep the words. Can I keep the words? I know the names of the whole team now! Is that alright, Emil?"

"That is very fine of you, Bela." He ducks his head in that endearing way of his whenever he is embarrassed by kindness.

The gypsy boy has no need for the words so agrees, but will not shake hands with Bela for fear of catching AIDS from strangers. As Bela carefully tears out the photos, the boy tells me how the dog ran across the lower circles of the *saracacios* and into the trees backing onto a distant building site not ten minutes ago.

Bela and I set off, zigzagging between the shacks as we slip down the slope into an empty pitch where bulldozers have cleared away the squatters for the new housing. Ahead of us, the shanties peter out under the shadows of unoccupied twelve-story apartment buildings with broken windows and soon we are back in the city. As we cross the subdued Piata Victorei, watched by militia in an armoured vehicle waiting for the curfew, I begin to worry that we may have to get off the streets and come back tomorrow night. By then, the dog may have been run down by the rag-ear gangs or one of the other rival hunters, freelance like myself. We know the rag-ears are about this evening, for at one point Bela finds the remains of a mutilated police horse, its body lying with shopping carts in the stagnant canal water, the head skinned of its *fado*. However, we must be lucky tonight, for near the presidential museum, I hear the dog again. I slap Bela on the back and we chase it past the foreign department stores of the South Zone, close enough to hear it padding nervously a street over.

"*Reusita*! It is going for the Palace of Justice!" I whisper to Bela. Bela knows a short-cut that brings us quickly to the July 14 Square, and as we enter the grand empty space, I spot it, nosing the trash left by the tourists on the steps of the Palace. We are just by the bus depot, not a hundred yards from the dog and less than two hundred from its nearest exit. Certainly close enough. I slip off the dart gun and load it while Bela tries to suppress his exhilaration by jamming his hands between his knees.

I crouch by an ice cream stall, take aim, taste the moment – but not for any personal triumph. This is only a poor trapped creature, dimly aware of how it has been tracked and outmanoeuvred. I have never understood those hunters who claim to enjoy the thrill of this instant, the rush in seeing an animal brought down as if the world could narrow to a single contest. When I went hunting on the plains with my father as a boy, he taught me that the true pleasure is to be had in knowing that we are only instruments of the animal's fate. As the dog jerks at my single shot, stumbling a few yards before collapsing from the drug, I reflect how my will and abilities have been loaded by unannounced forces, priming my life for moments like this. To think otherwise would be a terrible dishonour to the dog's memory, for how could I consider myself any less a part of the wider scheme than the animal itself.

Afterwards, with only a few minutes before the curfew, we collect the dog and hurry out of the square, Bela yelping with the body over his shoulder. It is too late to go to Marta's, so I lead Bela between the great shore hotels and cross the expressway to the beach. There, safely out of sight under the boardwalk, my hands deftly search the animal's fur until I find the marks – on the belly between the legs, unscarred by the dart's point of entry in the flank.

Excellent. Damaged goods would have got me less, repairs would have increased my expenses. I could not have hoped for it to have been in better condition.

"I knew you would find the dog, Emil," Bela says, frisking the unconscious animal above the ears. He starts murmuring, "*Don't speak to me of* fado, *no* sire, *tell me about the love.*"

"The other way around, Bela."

"Emil?"

"It goes: *do not speak to me of* love, *tell me about the* fado."

"Oh yes, Emil! The *fado*! *For* fado *is my sentence, and I was born to be lost.* That is how it goes, isn't that right, Emil?"

Grinning crazily, Bela scratches the dog's ears as if he has been given his first pet. From the way he moves his head from side to side, I can tell he would like his ears to be scratched as well, yet his ears are so tiny, quite ridiculous on a man as large as Bela. With his block torso and long arms, Bela's frame has had such confidence in its own momentum that it has never needed ears to listen out for what could be ahead. If so, his body had misjudged badly. For if I had not come across Bela two months ago, he would have careened into some invisible wall sooner or later.

Bela had been living on the streets by the soccer stadium, hanging out with a gang of gypsy boy prostitutes who kept him as a mascot and as protection from the citywide pimps. A casual listening would have clipped the rest of Bela's life – AIDS eventually (even if he was not a prostitute yet), or working the dumps to the south of the city, or employed by a neighbourhood credit syndicate as muscle until the *securistii* came for him. No doubt, dead before his third decade.

It was luck that I found him, buying him off his patrons and taking him on as an assistant, but I suppose my father would say it was part of that grander order that binds us both. Whichever, I am glad I did discover Bela – the alternative would have been a terrible waste.

"Bela?"

"Yes, Emil," he answers, smoothing the fur along the dog's back.

"We should finish."

With a nod, Bela puts both hands round the dog's neck and kills it with one sharp twist. I take the shaver from the tool bag Bela carries and check that I am right about the animal's belly. I am – it was not really a question – but without the fur, I can rub the thin grooves in the skin. The closely-packed concentric circles ripple outwards for three inches, branded deep into the flesh. My fingers touch the pattern and stroke it gently along the thin channels, and for a full minute, neither Bela nor I speak as we listen to the song playing softly under my hand.

"This is a good one, isn't it, Emil?"

I smile at him – he is getting much better at appreciating our pelts – but there are no words to communicate my feelings. The *fado* is too deep for speaking.

❖ ❖ ❖

It is pet's day at the *Muzsikas*.

To get into the bar on the Downtown outskirts, I have to push through a line of formally-dressed gypsies crowding the small corridor, its walls daubed with fluorescent *fado* circles and telephone numbers, and ease past dogs on the ends of rope leashes, stray cats held tightly by gypsy girls in their First Communion dresses, terrified pigeons quivering in bird cages too small for them. Each animal has the special marks – the corrugated surface of rings – which their owners finger hopefully as they wait to move forward into the club.

Inside, DJ Nick-Nick has organized one of his famous disc-cutting sessions. The dance floor has been covered with picnic blankets and in the middle, two veterinary school students are putting the animals to sleep with injections and slicing the *fado* from the pelts on the bar tables with surgical tools borrowed from a hospital. The carcasses are disposed of in large canvas sacks which the *Muzsikas* staff haul outside while hired craftsmen press the *fado* onto vinyl backings on Nicolae's private equipment and sand the edges of the discs. The air stinks of glue and burnt plastic. On an upper floor, the gypsies stand outside the DJ's turntable dais and wait for Nicolae to play a few seconds of each record, giving full concentration to each song before deciding which he will buy.

"Greetings, Emil!" Nicolae hails down when he sees me. "Anything for me?"

Nicolae will buy from anyone – even cast-offs from the rag-ears – and I have supplied him regularly over the years, but he only uses the *fado* to mix with dance records for the tourists on his club weekends. "No, not today," I tell him. I do not say that what I have this time is for a more discerning buyer.

"No Bela?"

"I have special business," I say, remembering Bela's crestfallen face when I told him he could not come this time. "Have you found anything?" I ask, nodding at the hopeful gypsies.

Nicolae scowls at the pile of discs beside the turntable. "Why do they always bring me cats? Easier to catch I suppose, but their *fado* are just too noisy, too – lazy! No *hunger* in the music. Maybe a few where you can hear the song, but." His hand cuts the sentence off with a gesture of resignation. "Some days, you get nothing pure, you know how it is, Emil."

"The plight of all collectors, Nicolae." Pure *fado* is indeed difficult to find. In the ten years since they first appeared, the tell-tale skin marks have been found all over the city, but few have the melody, and fewer still the true song – that *fado* that can blur the boundary between listener and music and blot the world out for a moment.

We talk a while longer about the state of the market and the fickle tastes of the tourists before Nicolae returns to his gypsies. I take a drink from Sandor behind the bar and find a chair that has not been stacked on a table. It is early yet, so I have time to sip my beer and watch people come into the club. In spite of the noise, the bar has a few customers: off-duty militia, *tauraf* of musicians with their instruments in cases, salesmen trying to forget their day.

After fifteen minutes, a prostitute enters the bar, receiving insults from the gypsies as she bangs her way through with a bulging shoulder bag so heavy it almost drags along the floor. She ignores them and starts to pass from table to table, speaking briefly with the customers. Some here know the woman – they fumble their beers nervously – but all dismiss her, sometimes politely, more often with an angry word. She accepts the refusals silently, picking up her bag and moving onto the next table in an arc that takes her around the bar.

When she reaches my table, I decide to speak first and save her the humiliation of asking. "I do not want to fuck. Go away."

The woman continues to stand in front of me, her head slightly bowed, staring at her worn shoes, as if she has not heard what I have said. I am about to repeat myself when she says, almost inaudibly, "*Domnule*, please. Listen to my song."

*My song*. The realization that this woman is not a prostitute prickles down my back, making me push my chair back and regard her carefully. Now I can see she looks like an office worker – mid-twenties, pretty enough in a white blouse and black knee-length skirt, with her unusually neat black hair in a bob and a little lipstick to brighten her face. I cannot see her eyes, but from the lines in her face, the rigid cast of the mouth, I wonder how long she has been going into bars, lugging the bag with her.

It would be a simple kindness to indulge her so I tell her to sit. Even before she heaves the case onto my table, I know what is there. She has trouble lifting out the portable record player but I do not help her, understanding that this is a ritual that she has performed many times before and must do without help. The player is a new model, but its silver casing is battered and it lacks a bass knob. There must be batteries in the back because the woman presses a switch at its side and the machine warms up.

Then from a side pocket of her bag, she pulls out the record – just smaller than a seven-inch, unlabelled, one side grooved, the other smooth vinyl. I can tell it is slightly warped as she takes it from its dirty sleeve and lays it on the rubber mat of the player. She lifts the player arm to start the record revolving, places the needle down on the dried skin surface and sits back in her chair with her hands carefully folded in her lap.

We listen. She will not look at me so I close my eyes – how else can I listen to it? A *fado* will be clear and powerful enough to sweep the world from me, so why not embrace the song immediately. And I have no doubt that this woman's record is strong *fado*.

Very quickly, the tune pierces the noisy world, dislocating it, and I am inside the *fado*. In a hot room, the heating is broken and the water pipe is slowly scalding the painted wall. While the light bulb flares as if it is about to burn out. And the woman is crooning in a wavery, off-key voice. Lying on a bed in which she has often lain but rarely slept, surrounded by young families, bickering already, in the new, crumbling apartment blocks. Singing her one song, clinging to the song as the one thing she can trust with her weight, putting in the words when she knows them, humming across the gaps. With her eyes wide open but no longer able to take anything in, either out of charity or self-preservation. For the woman believes that if she keeps singing this song, she can bear the sound of the man slipping away without saying goodbye. Such a tiny sound, the door shuts with barely a sigh, but it rattles all the way down her heart. Is it really that deep, such a big hole? But no tears, the song will hold them off until later, and maybe if she never stops singing, there will never be any later. So she sings of a woman who has been left, who will be left, who is always left alone, and however deep she will try to root her vows never to cheat or be cheated again, it will happen again, and again, as she and the world grind against each other, like an ignorant dance, like broken limbs, and the only thing to join them across their breach will be the song. Until it is over.

At last, I let out my breath. Very sad. Of course, the woman must be very proud of her record. Is the song the past or a glimpse of her future? In the mystery of *fado*, it is all the same. Listening to *fado* is like a part of the world being uncovered, the discovery of a hard and unbroken line that runs through it. Most people live across these lines and can drift between them, their *fados* muddy with the noise of an unfocused life that wanders without direction or record across the world. But the lucky ones – they exist *on* the lines, and have no choice but to hold to the line as it draws true to its target. Their lives are compressed into a song, and they can sing it with satisfaction or grief, but they must sing it to the end.

When the needle has been scratching back and forth at the centre for a full minute, the woman finally replaces the record in its sleeve and turns the player off. She puts it back into the bag and steps away from my table.

“Thank you”, barely whispered, is all she says.

Before leaving, the woman reaches up with her free hand to pull the black wig off her head and show me the scarred patch where she has been scalped for the *fado*. As she does so, the woman gives me a proud look, for no matter how bitter her song is, filled with curses at the infidelity of men and the weakness in her that drives her back to be betrayed time after time, there is an indescribable comfort in knowing that there is a fate that has been specially shaped for her.

For that is the joy of *fado*.

An hour after she has gone, the rag-ears finally arrive – two of them, preceded by a subtle rearrangement of the gypsies in the corridor as they part for the newcomers. The rag-ears are two boys, probably about thirteen, *gangsteri* dressed in fine American bomber jackets and expensive high-tops, paid for by the wealthy collectors to whom they have been indentured. Their ears are covered by felt hats pulled low over their heads, but the occupants of the bar stir restlessly nevertheless, coughing, shifting in their seats, tugging their jackets tighter. Of the many rumours about the rag-ears and their abilities, the one that frightens people most is the belief that they can hear the secrets of a life from the normal rustling of the body.

The rag-ears stalk the bar, and when they are satisfied they have marked the territory, they choose a table and wait for Sandor to bring them beers. I get the attention of one of the small *orfani* who carry messages between tables in tin cans and write a note. "Take this to the *gangsteri*," I tell the boy and pay him. When the rag-ears have read the note, they beckon me over.

"So you are the *fadisto*," the first one says. His sneer is mere bravado, so I concentrate on his colleague's expression. That look could be either admiration for a fellow talent or jealousy that I should be the one to find their prize. Ever since I had heard the news from one of my market sources that an unnamed minister in the government was seeking a certain melody, a special *fado* for his refined collection, I have been in competition with the rag-ears to find the pelt first. I would like to believe that my success was predestined.

"Do you have the song?"

"I do."

"But you do not carry it."

"Can you not hear it off my skin?" I tease them though I am nervous at their animal unease. "The echo of it in my hair?"

The second rag-ear takes off his hat, releasing long black hair, which he pulls aside to reveal the altered ear. Pinned back, the fleshy rim and lobes are as large as my hand and studded with dozens of small reverberators. Polished brown bone – the rag-ears' amplifier – spirals into the inner ear, and as I stare at it, I can almost see the bone vibrate faintly as the rag-ear listens to me deeply.

Within a few seconds, the rag-ear is grinning and calls to Sandor for more beers. "How much?" When I give him my price, he frowns, "So little, *fadisto*?"

"The *fadisto* does not do this for money, Fonica," the other says, leering at me as he listens to the distant barking of dog *fado* on Nicolae's turntable. "Can you not hear it on him?"

"What, Vladimir?"

"I do it for *fado*," I tell them both and order another beer from Sandor.

❖ ❖ ❖

"When are they coming, Emil?"

"Soon, Bela."

Bela rests his chin on his knees and starts rocking back and forth against the back wall of the *Muzsikas*. "It will be those rag-ears, won't it, Emil?"

"Yes, Bela," I say patiently.

"I do not like the rag-ears, Emil." Bela half-bites his kneecap. "They are like wild dogs."

When I do not answer him, Bela mumbles to himself, "*Don't speak to me of* fado, *but tell me about love.*" I would correct him, but Bela is nervous, saying the next line, "Fado *is my sentence*," over and over as if it is a lullaby that will calm him.

By my watch, it is seven o'clock, the right time, but the wide expanse of the Piata Victorei has few stragglers after hours. Another five minutes go by, and Bela becomes more restless, but then I hear the signal – a savage yell that startles the Piata's remaining pedestrians, making them hurry away.

"That is them, Emil?"

"Yes. You remember what to do with the dog pelt?"

Bela nods emphatically to show that I can trust this important job to him and grips the package close to his chest.

I take a deep breath, shivering. "Are you cold, Emil?"

"It is nothing, Bela."

"Emil, take my coat. I do not need it, my body is hot. Super-hot!"

Before I can desist him, Bela has taken off the thick long coat he nearly always wears and drapes it over my shoulders. Such kindness. I have tried to return it as best I could. Small things. Normally, at my insistence, he has heavy bandages around his torso to stop the rash from spreading down his chest. Tonight though there are no bandages under the coat. Again, at my insistence.

"Better, Emil?"

"Yes, thank you, Bela."

Smiling, Bela stands up and lopes out onto the street, looking down at his feet as if this is the only way he can appear non-chalant. I want to look at my feet too, but my ears will not let me and I have to stare at Bela's back – at the overlapping rings that gouge his skin, looping over his shoulder, around his ribs, down his spine, now singing out to the whole world without the cover of the bandages. Such *fado* I have never before seen crowded into a single body.

As soon as he puts the package down by the lamp-post, Bela turns to scurry back to me but the rag-ears are upon him before he can stand up. Bela has a massive build, but there are too many of them, rag-ears screeching as their hats tumble and roll across the street. Bela tries to stand, carrying the weight of six of the boys, but four more pull him down, and another four hold his arms to be handcuffed, and another four secure a leg for the one with a hypodermic, and another four step out of the mail van that pulls around the corner. Poor Bela screams out once – my name, of course – but it is muffled by the bodies on top of him and drowned by the sound of his *fado*, reaching its climax.

As they drag his body into the van, they sing perfectly in gorgeous voices, "*If you want to be my man, and always have me by your side, don't speak to me of love, but tell me about* fado. Fado *is my sentence. I was born to be lost.*"

I do not have to watch this, and through the tears, it is difficult, but how can I resist. The sight of a man discovering the truth of his destiny and giving in to its overwhelming force – is this not the beauty of *fado*?

Such satisfaction – especially when the *fado* is one's own.

That evening and every evening for the following week, I go to the *Muzsikas* and drink until she comes back again. I do not know if she recognizes me when she asks if I would hear her song, but I do not think she cares. She has lived with the *fado* for so long that nothing else matters.

When I have listened to her song, I put my hand on hers and tell her that she must hear mine now. As we lie in her bed afterwards, I ask her to trace the lines of the circles just beneath my shoulder-blades.

"Is its song not beautiful?"

The most precious sound in the world. A traitor's song. For my *fado* is to betray, and there is no sound more exquisite than the consummation of my destiny, fulfilled at last. And she nods, and sings her song to herself as I slip our of the bed and prepare to leave.

JOHN GOHORRY

# Project Butterfly

*I do not know whether I was then a man dreaming I was a butterfly, or whether I am now a butterfly dreaming I am a man* – Chuang Tse

*A butterfly flaps its wings in Beijing, and a week later there are storms over New York* – René Thom

## I

During the first year of his imprisonment in the work camp at Xien-lie, Chu Tse had some time to reflect on the question *What nourishes a man in captivity*? The implications of the prison diet and the backbreaking squalor of forced labour in the brickworks were clear from the outset. He must have enough food to sustain life and to fuel whatever work was required of him, enough rest to recuperate for the next day's labour. In such respects, his needs now were different in degree but not different in quality from those he had enjoyed as a free man.

But the mind craves its nourishment too, or the prisoner becomes that lesser thing which it is the goal of imprisonment to reduce him to – an obedient instrument, the agent not of his own apprehensions and purposes but of those in whose name the prison and the very codes of right and wrong that set it up were established.

Three things kept his spirit alive. One was an active imagination, which during the years of servitude would renew and re-shape his relationships with ideas, day to day, and so keep him free. Another was the public support of his friends, whose vigils and campaigns not only kept him alive in the eyes of the State and of the world at large, but also asserted his membership of the State as a whole and of the world as a whole beyond the prison confines. Third was the belief that though the State thought him expendable, he would eventually regain his freedom. He sustained this belief despite setbacks and encouragements during the last seven years of the

Deng regime. He wrote to Deng once a month, eighty-nine letters in all, although none was ever answered, and he continued to write, with renewed conviction, to the new leadership.

Others who lacked one of these three qualities did not survive so long, despite privileged rations. Fu Wei, a fellow dissident from Szechuan, had lost faith in his eventual freedom, and hence the will to live. Li Peng, a poet from Heinan, had no friends outside, and despite fifty two months of the most astonishing creative activity (he had improvised verses daily to Chu Tse and some other inmates), could achieve freedom of sorts only by hanging himself from his bunk using a torn sheet for a noose. As for Xang Hue, an electrician from Guangdong, at some point his creativity faded. He spoke only of the *chk chshsk* of a piston deep in the boiler room, its mechanical wheeze and thump imprinted so firmly that it took over his mind. The guards shot him on his way to the boiler room one night after curfew, after he had become a machine.

When the police hauled him out of his laboratory in the aftermath of Tiananmen Square, Chu Tse had had no time to collect his papers, no chance to conclude what had begun, twenty-two hours before, as a crucial experiment. Caesium pulsed in the compression chamber; strontium scattered its isotopes through a lead-lined alembic saturated with vapourised iodine, and in the vessel connecting them negative forces separated and converged in arrays constantly varied by a randomly changing electromagnetic field. A notebook of observations, a thick sheaf of calculations lay to hand on the bench. But the experiment was abandoned, running to its conclusion unobserved because Chu Tse, handcuffed with lightning rapidity, was frogmarched out of the building and into a van that took him to the interrogators. His papers were swept hurriedly into a plastic bag, surfacing briefly to form part of the prosecution evidence at his trial the following day, and although he continued, for the sake of principle, to demand their return in his monthly letter to the authorities, he realised long ago that even if they had escaped shredding or burning he would never see them again.

In the first months of his imprisonment he grieved bitterly over the loss of his papers and the frustration of a crucial experiment, but a turning point came in a talk he had oddly enough with Fu

Wei, who asked some specific outsider's questions about the nature of Chu Tse's research. This had the effect of focusing Chu Tse's attention on substantive aspects of his research rather than on the catastrophe of its having been halted, and Fue Wei proved a challenging and interested partner in conversation. Fu became a willing accessory to Chu Tse's acts of recollection, explanation and redefinition, so much so that the latter was, a few steps at a time, able to piece together most of the jigsaw of his past knowledge. "Thus *shi* (courage) overcomes *xu* (deficiency)," Fu Wei reflected one evening. Taking a small stick of bamboo he sketched the characters *hu* and *die* on the sand of the exercise yard and exhorted his friend to *think of the butterfly*.

That thought lodged in Chu Tse's mind, feeding and nourishing itself on the attention he gave it, not only in further talk with Fu Wei but in his own silent or near-silent musings over the course of time. No day passed without him devoting some hours to Project Butterfly.

At first he was not successful. An experiment that he had conducted three years before ran itself over and over again in his mind, achieving such overwhelming clarity in his memory that when he recalled any detail of it, the whole of the remainder was simultaneously present in his conception too, like the hologram of an event or an entire DNA profile expressed in a thread of hair. A formula that had enabled him to pass from the conclusion of one set of calculations to the opening premises of another remained locked in oblivion whatever conscious manoeuvres he tried to extricate it with.

Yet slowly he repossessed what he knew. With the advantage of hindsight he was spared some of the inconvenience that attends those who must find a way, and he could sometimes economise his efforts of recollection, choosing not to pursue lines of thought that he sensed were blind alleys. This set of calculations was complete. That was expendable. In a couple of years he had reconstituted the foundations of his research.

In the course of this reconstruction, certain new lines of enquiry suggested themselves. He had set these aside at the time, but he was now free to consider them, and as the months passed he devoted the core of his mind to the enlargement of each in turn. About this time, certain changes occurred in his psycho-sensual constitution. His sense of smell became extraordinarily acute, and he became afraid of birds.

His aroused sense of smell was extremely troublesome, since everything about the prison stank. Arriving at Xien-lie all those years ago he had been nauseated by the foul air of the place, but it had become familiar, tolerable even. Now it was worse than ever. The stink of his fellow prisoners, the reek of the prison buildings – bunkhouse, canteen, latrines – all this was intensified, and his range of sensation increased dramatically as well. He smelt the flesh of a dead rat two hundred yards from the source and the sweet hint of death itself in the pit of Fu Wei's lungs on the other side of the exercise yard, though his eyes were still full of life as he drew near. There were compensating sensations as well – the smoking unfolding of the land after rain, the sour exhalations of a fern. He caught a glimpse, once, of a young woman rumoured to be the Governor's daughter, and drew deep draughts of her warm, intimate scent as she stepped in a scarlet dress out of his limousine and made her way to the doors of the Brick Factory office, half a mile to the east.

The sky troubled him. Ravens loomed out of nowhere, circling from the back of his head and performing grotesque manoeuvres in the air before him. He smelt the scrofulous pit of their underwings, the grubby residues of beak, claw and feather, and he shrank from their awkward descent and the cold incurious swagger with which they moved towards him. Smaller birds, sparrows and starlings, startled him with their sudden clamouring, the quick, darting movements that they made about him and which he had no power to control.

He mentioned these things to Fu Wei, who said merely that they were perfectly normal symptoms of his development and that he should continue what he had started.

## II

Though neither Deng nor his ministers ever formally answered the Chu Tse's letters, after three months of imprisonment he was allotted a short, supervised visit from a member of his family once every six weeks. No physical contact was permitted during these visits, and no transactions were allowed; it was therefore impossible for anything material – books, food, medicines, messages – to pass between visitor and inmate. Only words might be exchanged, and those words spoken in a quiet interview room staffed by guards set to listen.

The journey from Beijing to Xien-lie was long and difficult, but every six weeks Chu Tse's fiancée, Q'ing Lai, had travelled to see him. They had spent twenty minutes together in the interview room under the eyes and ears of the guards, and then she had left. It was an established pattern, from which both derived comfort. Q'ing Lai was distressed very much, though she did her best to conceal it, when after two years of her visits, Chu Tse asked if she would arrange for him to see his cousin Shu. This distressed her because visits from Cousin Shu could only be at the expense of her own time with Chu Tse, but she knew something must be afoot since Cousin Shu was proverbial among the family for one very remarkable attribute – his prodigious memory. Shu's memory was incredible. He recalled the days of particular dates with unfailing accuracy, and could memorise lists of great length with no evident difficulty. He was a reliable source of information on bus timetables, monthly production figures, fluctuations in temperature, the sequence of stations on most rail routes through the northern half of the People's Republic.

Cousin Shu realised early on in the first visit what was required of him. He sat at the dirty table opposite Chu Tse as the guards hovered and watched them with stony, impassive eyes. Chu Tse asked for news of the family, which Shu gave as well as he could. Shu asked for his part about conditions on the inside, and Chu Tse talked about his food, his accommodation, his work in the Brick Factory. He told Shu about his acute sense of smell, his apprehensions of birds. The two men would sometimes sing briefly together, recalling snatches of old songs. Then Cousin Shu would depart.

Chu Tse found plenty of opportunities to quantify information. He gave indications of the size and weight of his food, the dimensions of buildings, his output of bricks day by day. He described the exact spiralling motions of the ravens.

Yielding place on occasions to Q'ing Lai, Cousin Shu made over thirty visits to Chu Tse over the next five and a half years, and at the end of each visit made a sheaf of neat annotations, setting down the expression of quantities conveyed to him by Chu Tse. From small beginnings it had quickly become possible to express a wide range of mathematical relations, from *is greater/less than* and *equals* to *is included in, to the power of,* and *transforms to*. Even if he did not immediately pick up every mathematical nuance of the codes in which Chu Tse spoke to him, Cousin Shu's prodigious memory enabled him to reflect, week after week, on the enigmas of what had been said.

Chu Tse's health deteriorated over those five and a half years, but his determination did not slacken, nor did the vigilance of the guards. Then Deng died, and with his sentence unmitigated by the new régime, Chu Tse asked Cousin Shu to remember him especially to his cousin, Wu Chen, who worked in one of the factories in the Shanghai Economic Zone. On other occasions he asked after a nephew, Sun Bin, expressing particular concern at his progress now that he had passed his school examinations and was starting work. This Cousin Shu took as a sign that he must act as there was no child of that name in the family and the only Sun Bin Cousin Shu knew of was the Classical writer on military strategy.

## III

Wu Chen settled comfortably alongside his manager, MacWherry, on the midweek Air China flight out of Hongquiao airport, bound for New York. It was almost a decade since Stanford Electronics, of Paterson, New Jersey, had set up a joint venture in Shanghai, taking advantage of the low overheads and favourable tax conditions guaranteed in the new Economic Zones in return for overseas capital investment, expertise and technology. Ten years ago, Stanford's technology had been state of the art, but advances in resonance imaging in the interval had convinced MacWherry of the need to reinvest. As a senior member of the production team,

Wu Chen would outline the positive impact of upgraded technology on the purchase of raw materials, product scheduling, and quality of finished goods, which would keep Stanford ahead in the fast developing markets of the Pacific Rim. Together, they hoped to persuade the parent company.

The flight from Shanghai to New York took over 20 hours. At the beginning, Wu Chen and MacWherry kept one another alert with a discussion of how they would present their case; as the plane moved out over the interminable eastern edge of the North Pacific, each lapsed into the privacy of his own thoughts. First Wu Chen, then MacWherry slipped off into a sound sleep. Wu Chen dreamed of confinement in a long, cigar-shaped container full of bracken and tree roots, a dark, warm, fertile place heaving with maggots and insect life, which was furiously occupied in the search for a gold nugget buried somewhere deep in the forest floor. When he woke, he was utterly famished, and accepted the pretty stewardess's offer of a full evening meal, which he ate heartily.

As the plane flew with the spin of the earth eastwards, night came to them quickly. Wu Chen brooded during the brief darkness on the nugget that lay under the forest floor, on his projected production schedules, on the papers his Cousin Shu had asked him to carry with him, in the greatest secrecy, to the proper authorities. He slept fitfully again, for some hours. Now the plane dropped into Anchorage to refuel he breathed a deep sigh of relief. Cousin Shu had assured him that his trip to New York would not be scrutinised. The authorities, preoccupied with the repossession of Hong Kong and the Territories, would be looking to the south, and he would be able to "cross the sea without Heaven's knowledge". Then the plane drove on and on eastwards through the five time-zones of North America, and at half-past seven in the evening of the same day they had left Shaghai, Wu Chen and MacWherry landed at Kennedy Airport.

They had talks with their people in Paterson the next couple of days, and MacWherry went off on the Saturday to visit relations in Chicago. This left Wu Chen plenty of time to take a short flight down to Washington, where he visited Capitol Hill, climbed the

Washington Memorial, and handed Chu Tse's calculations over to the guards manning Security Access to the Pentagon.

## IV

A week later three meetings occurred. In the Project Office of Stanford Shanghai there were celebrations at a fax from the States confirming investment in $3m worth of resonance imaging technology. MacWherry spoke of the benefits that this would bring – the assurance of future contracts, the lead Stanford would keep over their competitors, their enhanced reputation for quality products. He paid tribute to Wu Chen for the valuable part he had played in discussions with the parent company. Wu Chen spoke of the difference the new technology would make to production processes, and of the challenges ahead that they would welcome, with its support, bringing excellence to their business.

In the Westmoreland Briefing Room at the Pentagon, General Powell addressed his Defence Strategists. The papers of Chu Tse had been closely examined by a group of eminent scientists including Ducaine, Parisi, and the Nobel prizewinner, Vogelsang. Their conclusions were unanimous. He guessed everyone knew Einstein's $E = mc^2$, even if they didn't know how it was arrived at. What Vogelsang and the others had discovered was that at the very highest energy levels, Einstein's formula became the same sort of rough and ready approximation that it had shown Newton's to be. It explained the existence of black holes, but it couldn't account for what went on inside them.

They had worked on the mathematics of an alternative for a number of years without success. Chu Tse's calculations, which stemmed from a quite different starting point – General Powell, glancing at the mathematicians' report, picked out the names Gödel, Euler, and Boscovich – gave a reasoned account of the energy transfers within black holes, and made a number of inferential suggestions about the behaviour of particles in the fractions of time immediately before Big Bang.

In the interview room at Xien-lie, Q'ing Lai fought back her tears as she sat once again opposite Chu Tse. She had not seen him for almost six months, and in this time he had greatly aged. His eyes were set deep in their sockets, and the skin was drawn tight at his temples and over the crown of his head. Networks of purple veins stood out on the back of his hands like the signature of some still undefined state of affairs that was working its way towards diagnosis. She sensed that at last he was breaking free from the shackles of circumstance that confined him, and when she realised this, she was glad.

PENNY SIMPSON

# Smoking Wills

## *(i) Pearls and Prophecies*

Maria Pasovic struggled across the pot holed road to reach the solicitor's office. There was a tram strike and she had already wasted precious hours queuing for a loaf of stale bread in the market on the Bulevar Octobarske Revolucije. She was late for her three o'clock appointment and she could sense Boujan would be chiding her. Maria had no doubt that her recently deceased husband would still be kicking ass – even in the afterlife – but it was her ass she was most concerned about that afternoon. For Boujan's will promised to be as explosive as his fits of temper, which had punctured their thirty years of married life together like so many collapsed balloons.

Boujan's ugly temper had only ever had one advantage as far as Maria could see: it had been a ballast in a world where everything else resembled the road stretching out before her – one full of craters, ready to send you spinning into black holes of distrust and confusion. The small widow was worried that this meeting with her solicitor Nikolai Petrovic might prove to be yet another black hole waiting to catch her falling body. Maria had always been nervous of officials of any description. Because of her fears, she had long ago developed the habit of ravelling the threads of her family life up into a carpet of secrecy that could lie undetected by even the nosiest of her neighbours. She was so good at saying nothing, that she could recite her litany of harmless domestic woes for hours at a time standing in the city's endless food queues. Her tongue on these occasions was always busy, although her feet were forced to remain still.

– How can you cook these potatoes, neighbours? – the blight on them is like a second skin . . . Salad? call this a salad? These leaves are the colour of snot . . . Pay how much for a bar of soap?

Cretins! This soap works itself up into less of a lather than my Boujan when he has lost money gambling . . .

– I can't argue with you, Maria, Boujan muttered as she unfolded the latest domestic crisis.

– You would stop a saint from finding sense in your ramblings.

His wife's replies would be laced with the sarcasm she could only give vent to behind the sanctuary of their closed doors.

– We may have our freedom, but look: we still queue to sit down in our own home!

Maria was irritated that Boujan always got to relax in their comfortable chair. This padded swivel leather armchair had been looted from an office during the most recent Revolution to take place in their upside-down country and Boujan had from the first dominated its collapsing springs. Maria still had to ease her queue-weary feet sitting down on the old kitchen stool.

– See if he doesn't get the last laugh in their interminable argument of a marriage.

So mocked Ines Boric, the Pasovic's closest neighbour. He had lived almost as long as the arguing couple had done in the crowded riverside tenement situated off the Boulevard. Like many others, he had taken up prophecy after the Revolution. He delivered his orations from one of the new street kiosks that had sprung up round the Boulevard, which he ran whilst at the same time clutching an imported cheap cigarette between his black, crooked teeth. Smoking had always had a great impact on the nation's political health – as well as on the state of its citizens' molars. Before the Revolution, everybody had smoked on principle – a deeply held political principle. The government had tried to ban smoking on the grounds that it damaged people's health, so dissent was expressed by tobacco consumption on a scale that must have made somebody a tidy profit.

That person, as Maria knew only too well, was not her husband. Boujan had smoked incessantly until their tiny flat stank so much she couldn't even make out the scent of her favourite perfume. Maria had given her husband an ultimatum: either the cigarettes left the flat, or she would leave. Boujan backed down and she banned cigarettes from even being carried into her home. Her husband's friends would wait for him out in the corridor, packets of tobacco freshly purchased from Ines buried deep in their waistcoat pockets.

Boujan's teeth, like those of his friend Ines, were in an appalling condition. Indeed, it was the sight of his blackened molars that turned his daughter Natalie into a rebel rather than any of the dynamic changes occurring in the world of politics. From an early age, she had vowed she would keep her teeth as white as those displayed by the male models in the American magazines her civil servant friend helped smuggle into the city. Natalie pinned photographs of these tanned models with their gleaming white teeth all over the bathroom walls, but Boujan remained immune to their dental charms. He would spit into the tin bowl he used for his daily shave and denounce their manhood.

Natalie was not to be deterred from dreams of improving on the state of her all-too deficient molars. She dreamt of owning reams of dental floss, enough to build herself a rope that would stretch across to America. Here, everybody would concur that her teeth and her radiant smile were the best to be seen anywhere in the entire Western world. To further her ambitions, Natalie taught herself English from old novels she bought from the trading stalls ringing the Pasovics' tenement. She like tales of derring-do on the high seas, of women in crinolines abducted by highwaymen, but her favourites were the hospital dramas in which ill-health was a bonus, because it put you straight into the arms of miracle workers with large bank balances.

– I shall marry a plastic surgeon when I go to America, Mama. He will make your legs look like a showgirl's! No more of those funny bumps.

Maria hobbled out of the flat on the two legs her daughter found so disgusting. They were laced with dozens of painful varicose veins, but it was her daughter's dreams which made her cry at night. Somebody had told her that young people in America slept out on the streets and even in underground tunnels alongside rats and mad people. They were so poor, they traded out of their very pockets to stay alive. She did not want her child to ever experience such a fate.

Even in the worst of times, when neighbour had denounced neighbour, there had been no threat of the Pasovics' ever losing their home. It was undoubtedly because Boujan had always been feared, or to be more precise, his great gusts of temper had seemed to win them the immunity they needed from the battalions of spies who masqueraded as family friends in their seething tenement block. They had never been hauled up to the headquarters of the secret police, a small miracle in its own way, because those snakes had been very far from invisible in their neck of the woods. They had been crucial to the fabric of everyday life and you always knew them by the smart shoes they wore. Yes, Maria took a look down at people's shoes and knew at once who was to be trusted and who was to be avoided. Anybody who struggled to get by in life wore down-at-heel shoes, held together with string or shreds of cardboard, but the secret police always wore brilliantly shiny shoes. It must be a badge of entry, Maria had thought, as important as shooting a bull's eye on a moving target.

Prompted by these reflections, Maria took a discreet glance down at the footwear worn by the young solicitor seated before her. His shoes were made out of the most beautiful leather. Maria shivered and then she looked up and returned his gaze. He was so young, she wondered if he would ever be able to sort out Boujan's tangled will. Maria knew it would be complicated, because her husband had been forever changing its contents. Each domestic dispute would send him flying out of the door, brandishing his fists, screaming damnation upon poor Maria and Natalie, who really only wanted a little peace – and dental floss and stiletto shoes – to make life on the twentieth floor of their tower block that little more bearable. Maria settled down on one of the office's antique walnut chairs and plopped her old-fashioned handbag down onto her knees. It was the kind of handbag that came complete with a vicious clasp that put Maria's fingernails in danger whenever it snapped shut.

– Well, there is good news and there is bad news, Mrs Pasovic. Where would you like to start?

– I find the beginning as good a place as any, replied the indomitable little woman.

– Quite so. Your husband, Mrs Pasovic, was not a poor man. You must have had an inkling of that, but maybe you will be surprised at just how much he managed to salt away?

Maria, to tell the truth, was stunned at the news that Boujan had anything to hand over to his family. She had not thought there would be much left over once the solicitor's fees and the bribe for the undertaker had been paid. She swung her legs to and fro whilst she reflected on this unexpected piece of news. Nikolai bided his time. Inwardly, he had been surprised at the sight of Mrs Pasovic. She looked more like a wizened child than a grown woman. He waited patiently until Maria's legs came to a halt before proceeding to outline the exact contents of Boujan's will.

– Mrs Pasovic, your husband has left you £30,000. It's a magnificent sum.

– So, what's the catch?

Now the solicitor knew from his last meeting with Boujan all about the ban on smoking at home. He was trying to think of a tactful way of expressing the next part of Mr Pasovic's legacy, but he was also amused at the effect it might have on this little gnome-woman sitting in front of him.

– The catch, Mrs Pasovic, is that you must smoke *ten* cigarettes a day in order to inherit.

He didn't dare look at Maria after making his staggering announcement. Instead, he concentrated on her legs, which had once again taken up their swinging. They drummed against the antique walnut chair in a most agitated fashion and he was worrying about the damage they might cause when Mrs Pasovic suddenly burst across his train of thought.

– I have never smoked and I can't think how I would ever start smoking. And my daughter would not be keen either. She wants to spend her share of the money on dental floss.

– Those are the terms of your husband's will and they must be met with strictly before we can hand over any money.

– Then I shall have nothing.

– But Mrs Pasovic, reflect a moment: this is a small fortune. You could buy your own flat. You could join the ranks of the property-owning class.

– I will never smoke – not one little single cigarette. Even if I have to give up all I am owed, never will I smoke. The old devil. Tell me honestly, sir, do you think God allows smoking? May he rot up there, denied his horrible cigarettes, let him be forced to clean the Pearly Gates, as pearly as my Natalie's teeth . . .

Nikolai had lost her train of argument by this point, but it didn't matter for Maria was up on her feet and ready to leave. He ushered her out of his office – she was still delivering oaths up to her dead husband – and then shut the door behind her with a loud bang. He sat down on the walnut chair and laughed to himself. So what if she didn't take the money? His firm might well be able to cook up a claim to keep it in trust for the Pasovic estate. Under these circumstances, a large percentage of the inheritance might well come his way – enough maybe to buy his girlfriend the real diamond ring she was always going on about.

### *(ii) a call on Einstein*

The Pasovics' neighbours expressed their deepest sympathy for Maria's predicament when she returned home from the solicitor, but the minute her back was turned, they sniggered and snorted over her humiliation.

– All those years, she allowed him not one of his pleasures. It catches up with you in the end, crowed Natasha, Ines's wife.

She was a compulsive smoker too like her husband. Her lips were imprinted with two little groove marks from the never-ending succession of cigarette butts she smoked.

– But surely she can't resist for long? Natasha continued.

– Just a few cigarettes a day and think of all that money she stands to make. It's a sin to refuse in my book!

– Maria is determined to appeal, Ines interrupted her. She thinks she can win on health grounds.

The circle of neighbours crowded into the tenement's stairwell paused to think about the likelihood of such claims. They had all heard in the past the government's claims that lung cancer and heart attacks could be caused by smoking, but these had been ideas promoted by the old régime and how on earth were they to be trusted? Here they were creeping back into power with mint-new names, but previous little change in their ways of thinking. Natalie was initially her mother's sole supporter in the matter of the appeal. The grounds for success in her opinion relied on nothing more than the evidence of her clean, bright smile. She felt sure it would sway a judge in their favour if they ever got to court to challenge the legality of Boujan's demands. Her wonderful molars were even now being varnished to sparkling perfection thanks to the regular supplies of fluoride toothpaste she was buying from a black marketeer on the Boulevard.

Maria was not so sure about the way things were going. She still went on her morning rounds, queuing here, queuing there, and all the while she heard nothing but trouble from her neighbours. Rents had suddenly tripled in some parts of town overnight and with no explanation. People were crowding into relatives' flats to try and make ends meet. There was even less food in the shops, because those with spare cash, or government connections, were stockpiling anything nutritious. Her daughter's doubts only began to emerge when she got a pain in the side of her mouth.

– I think I have a wisdom tooth coming through, Mama, she said one night as they sat watching an Italian game show together on satellite television.

– Keep it safe. You will have need of some of that wisdom soon, her mother had replied.

– The way things are going, Einstein himself could not make sense of the changing prices in the shops.

Natalie's pain did not go away, however, and she began to fret that it might be a portent for a major dental tragedy. Her boyfriend Mikhail shrugged his shoulders and told her to wait and see.

– That's all we have ever done! I might die before I see anything I really want to see, Natalie snapped back.

He retreated behind his newspaper, so she began to badger her mother over the terms of Boujan's disputed will. Natalie's fears of pending dental catastrophe had prompted her to change tack on dealing with her father's proposal. Doctors and dentists would need bribing to treat her poisoned gums. She forgot about the fluoride and the floss and dreamt instead of accumulating dozens of bundles of dollar notes.

– Look, Mama, you smoke a little now and again and it really won't harm you. You have to smoke for forty, fifty years, before there is even a little bit of damage. Look at old Natasha. She's so fit and strong. I saw her carry two loads of washing up the stairs yesterday. She didn't so much as puff when she got to her door.

– And my teeth? asked her mother slyly.

– Oh, it's ages before nicotine starts really staining the enamel, you know that.

– You've changed your tune, Natalie.

But Maria understood her daughter's sense of alarm. There was still no date set for the appeal hearing and it might be months before they heard anything, because new elections were pending and the world was once again on the verge of being thrown up into the air like two dice. Where might that not lead? Who would be the new judges and the new politicians? Maria worried and fretted and finally she went back to see her solicitor.

– How exactly do you plan putting this absurd notion of my husband's into practice?

– There will have to be mediation of some kind, Nikolai replied.

In the end, they agreed on setting up a three-month trial period during which time Nikolai was to go round to the Pasovic's flat at a set time each day and watch the widow smoke her ten cigarettes. In return, the family would receive a quarter of Boujan's money up front to pay for the best city dentist to treat Natalie's sore gums. But the girl's predicament was more serious than they had at first realised. Her left gum was sore and a tooth was now visible, but there was also a growth on her tongue. Tests revealed it to be cancer. She must have treatment immediately. Maria, stung by guilt and panic in equal measure, agreed she could fly to an American clinic. Natalie for her part could not absorb the shock of having such awful news delivered to her by a consultant with only too visibly rotting teeth. She fell back on her fantasy world. In California, she would meet her dream-date doctor in a clinic she had seen featured in one of the magazines supplied by her civil servant friend. This doctor would perform a miracle in getting her well again and then they would appear in *Hello!* magazine by a swimming pool that stretched the length of Bulevar Octobarske Revolucije.

## *(iii) stilettos for a bald heroine*

Natalie's dreams were jolted when the hair on the back of her head began to fall out. She had not expected to deteriorate so visibly; it was not something that was ever mentioned in her cheap novels. There were no balding heroines between the pages of fiction. She had thought she might lose a little bit of weight, which truth to tell she had welcomed, but her hollow, pale face, dotted with red rashes, terrified her. When her mouth broke out in ulcers and she could hardly swallow, she wept again. Maria held her hand and said that the radiotherapy was nearly always successful in cases like hers. She was lying. She also took the precaution of hiding her daughter's mirror away in her capacious handbag. Soon, she was not even allowed to hold her child's hand. She was kept in isolation in the clinic, because the doctors had had to put radioactive rods into her tongue in a bid to burn away the tumour.

Natalie cried a lot more in her little white bed. She longed for physical contact, but the doctors and nurses were distant, dressed up in special gowns with plastic gloves. They were not human, they were certainly nothing like the blonde, curly-haired charmers found in Natalie's fictional world. Maria watched her daughter failing to eat and longed to feed her by hand, like she had when she was a baby and her digestion had been so bad they had had to make meals into a game. She tried to think up ways of persuading her to eat even the tiniest of morsels. All the while, the cancer treatment was eating up Boujan's money. Natalie, her face puffed up by the radiotherapy and by her tears, begged to go home to wait the results of her tests. Maria breathed a sigh of relief and booked two flights the following morning.

Home was drab and cold. The central heating had broken down and the tenants could not reach an agreement with the landlord on who was to be held responsible for paying the workmen. Maria retreated to the streets to search for fruit and vegetables to provide

Natalie with the ingredients for her special diet. The nurse at the clinic in California had been apologetic when she handed over the cancer diet recommended by Natalie's consultant.

– I think you will have to improvise a bit, Mrs Pasovic. The pineapple and mango juices, for example. An orange would be just as beneficial.

Maria had been incredulous as she lit up her twentieth cigarette of the day. Even one small orange cost a pretty penny in these times. They would have to introduce serious cutbacks if they were called back to the clinic for further treatment. Boujan's money had gone so far, but it was not going to stretch indefinitely if they kept up the rate of spending they had achieved in California. Maria made some more calculations on the back of an old cigarette packet. Natalie watched her from her father's old chair, which she had pulled up close to the apartment's open windows.

– Mama, I'm sorry.

– Why sorry darling?

– Look what I have done. It is all my fault. I wanted so much to go to America and to leave you. This is my punishment.

– Nonsense. Look, soon, I shall stop smoking. I think we have done more than enough to play along with your Dada's stupid ideas.

Three months after returning home, they received good news from the clinic in America. Natalie was in remission. Maria reflected on her daughter's diagnosis as she inhaled on her next roll-up. Rolling her own cigarettes had become yet another way of economising. She was able to buy brown bags of tobacco cheaply from Ines, who was delighted to find Maria as lucrative a customer as her husband had once been, particularly in these times of cut-throat competition. Maria discovered that she really liked the taste of her new tobacco, whilst its scent lingered in her home, like her perfume had once done. True, she wheezed a little now and again when the lift was broken and she had to climb up nineteen flights of stairs, but inspecting her teeth each morning, she could see that they were still unmarked by the cigarettes' nicotine. Natalie, however, remained unconvinced by her mother's change of heart. She burnt all her carefully hoarded fashion magazines and then she threw away her collection of designer cosmetics. Maria wailed when she saw her leave the house without her eyes made-up in kohl and eye shadow.

– So, you are going to end up looking like me?

– You are so good, Mama, I could never be like you.

Her daughter's sadness ate away at Maria's poor heart. She longed for the days when they had sat together looking at magazine advertisements, bidding against each other with beans to see who could win what in a fantasy game show they had invented to play when Boujan went out to drink with his friends. Those days had gone for ever, she realised. Nikolai still called round occasionally, although the trial period they had agreed on had long since expired, and he could not help but notice how every time he arrived at the flat, Maria was busy smoking one of her hand rolled cigarettes.

– Mrs Pasovic. You have let your husband win over you. Here you are, practically a chain smoker, he remonstrated one day.

– But I saved my daughter's life. You know, Nikolai, everybody has their fantasies. My husband would have enjoyed thinking about the impact of his little joke long before he died. And I enjoy my cigarettes. That was something he could never had foreseen, so I have won too. But sometimes, we lose out badly by trying to forecast the future. Take my daughter. She wanted the world, but she was looking at a phoney world. You and I know better; we strike a deal when we see how things are going. I'm not saying I don't dream – I'd love a washing machine, for example – but all the same my feet are staying firmly on the ground.

The solicitor looked down at his own rather splendid leather shoes planted squarely on the Pasovics' floral carpet. They were Gucci rip-offs, but leather all the same. He smiled a wry smile. Mrs Pasovic was no fool.

– Cigarette, Nikolai? I think I've got some Marlboro somewhere.

Maria rummaged in her black handbag to find the previous packet she had been hoarding for some special occasion. She lit up two cigarettes and handed one over to the solicitor, who had in the meantime made himself as comfortable as he could on her old kitchen stool. Both smokers inhaled deeply and then smiled at each other across the fumes.

– So, what next, Maria?

– I'm on the look-out for a pair of black stilettos for my daughter's birthday. Do you think you can help me?

ANNE LEWIS

# Emmanuel's Land

*Basseterre, Guadeloupe 1857*

Ten years have passed. La Carène has gone the way of so many old estates: divided up, no longer viable, its people scattered throughout the Islands.

I wonder if any of them still remember.

We were breaking ground on the headland when the boat appeared. At that distance it was no more than a faint blot, an ill-defined shadow against the quicksilver dazzle of strong morning sun on the sea. I crept closer, and acquired an identity: Maurice's leaky old fishing tub, so familiar it was hardly worth a second glance, except as a brief respite for cramped backs, a chance to hawk and spit and shift position. Why I went on watching it, I don't know.

Now I could make out the crazy-patched sail, the blotches of tar on the unpainted hull. The breeze carried voices up to us – Maurice and his son André – and I even fancied I caught a faint whiff of rancid fish oil from the bilges.

As it passed beneath the headland, the sail dropped. Oars poked out, and André began rowing towards the jetty. Only then did I see that there was a passenger aboard.

A white woman. Unescorted. Alone.

Others besides myself had seen it now. I was conscious of a collective shifting and straightening all around me, of low-voiced oaths expressing astonishment, of women calling out in excitement and children running to see what we were staring at. We all knew who she must be.

"*His woman*?" Matthieu's old voice was a tremulous croak. "She's *here*?"

Mattocks thumped to the ground forgotten and suddenly they were away – every man, woman and child, pelting off down the track to the jetty. Chains and whips might have held them, but I, who was one of them, and commanded neither, nor wished to – I was powerless to halt or deflect that mass exodus, that overwhelming compulsion to see, to press close, to touch. I could see people converging on the waterfront from every corner of the estate.

I stayed where I was. I watched the boat and its pale cargo inch its way across the creek, and I knew that I was wholly unprepared for this encounter. I wished with all my heart that she had stayed away.

Céline was beside me, her gaunt face expressing contempt.

"She's insane. No escort? Doesn't she care?"

I shrugged. "She's a stranger, perhaps customs are different in France. But Maurice should have known better. He's put our necks in a noose."

"I could take steps."

"No!" The implications chilled me. "No. Let her see what she wishes to see. I'll ride to the mission and fetch Père Martin to escort her back. He won't betray us."

She considered for a moment, and nodded.

But as we made our way down the track I heard her murmur, "She cannot take him away from us now."

He had left a half-finished letter – the last thing he ever penned. Père Martin had written to her, at my urging, enclosing it and explaining the circumstances. Some months afterwards he showed me her reply: a short note, kindly worded, grateful. And that should have been the end of it.

But then, over a year later, she had written directly to me. The letter was waiting for me, unopened, when next I called at the mission-house. Whoever had sorted the mail was evidently not aware that the M. Joseph Gautier to whom it was addressed was black, and at that time unfree.

She had secured a passage to Guadeloupe, she told me, and hoped to be with us in the spring.

That letter put me in a quandary. What should I do? Whom should I inform? By law I had no rights – not even the right to a private correspondence. I could take no action without referral to authority. Our present agent was a Creole, one of the old, lazy, unapproachable sort, comfortably domiciled in town and quite content to leave La Carène to manage itself as long as there were no irregularities to compel intervention. I knew him by reputation. He would be unsympathetic, to say the least; the whole issue would be misconstrued, hasty and ill-considered action would be taken and we would all suffer.

So I had let the matter ride. What else could I do? I could not even make enquiries at the port without arousing suspicion.

But here she was. Unannounced, solitary, unprotected, under the wing of that old renegade Maurice. It did not occur to me until later that she had planned it so.

She sat quite composed while André shipped the oars and Maurice threw a line ashore. I was astonished at how small she was, how slight, how fragile. Her very paleness was unexpected: startling in contrast with the dark river and that solid mass of black bodies waiting to greet her. Pale-brown hair beneath a straw hat; pale cotton dress sprigged with brownish flowers; skin like parchment. Not so much white as blanched, I thought – all colour bleached out, like sun-dried grass.

Maurice helped her ashore. The crowd pressed around her, every face alight with a mixture of elation and frank curiosity. Voices called out a babble of excited greetings, the women stretching their arms out to touch her dress and her hair and her white skin; the men, not daring to touch, grinning and bobbing and buffeting each other noisily on the back to relieve their feelings.

She stood there unresponsive. I suppose she was terrified. Her eyes searched the crowd in mute appeal and finally met mine, where I stood apart at the top of the ramp. And though we had never met, she smiled recognition.

Only then did she turn to the welcoming faces, and begin to grasp the hands which thrust at her from all sides, to repeat names, to embrace the children, to make her way slowly through the press towards Céline and me.

I had seen her described as cold. She did not seem so to me. All I saw in her face and her demeanour that day was a shy reserve, sweetness and a kind of amazed self-deprecation: "Why are they making such a fuss over *me*? – I wish they would not."

She looked up, first at me, then at Céline. And I saw an expression on her face so like his that my heart faltered. A rush of successive feelings, swift as flames: grief, compassion, relief, gladness.

"Joseph," she said, and extended both hands. "Céline." Even the smile was his, except that its luminosity was a little shadowed, like a reflection in a darker glass.

Céline said gruffly, "You are welcome, mademoiselle."

There had been no welcome for him when he arrived: no welcome at all.

We had a white overseer then: a drunken pig of a Boer. Elsewhere in the French Islands slaves were treated humanely. La Carène was the exception: an unacknowledged scandal. The estate was close to ruination – I learnt later that there had been a long-running dispute over inheritance.

We were chained in our work-gangs, shackled and locked in at night. The Boer abused the women, flogged the men, half-starved the children, and no-one intervened. We were no less brutish than he – how could we be, under such circumstances? Every night there was drinking, there was whoring, there were fights – and every dawn the sight of blood and vomit and the stench of raw spirits, and a thick aching head to cushion the harshness of the new day.

Until *he* arrived.

We heard the clatter of hooves in the yard just after sundown. Two horses. The overseer had ridden off that morning to make his report to the new agent in town. Evidently, he had brought someone back with him. Maybe a woman. It was no concern of ours.

We heard the sound of men dismounting. The Boer shouting for Céline. And then a man's clipped French voice demanding, "Where are your workers?"

In the sheds, ears pricked up. It was the new agent himself.

The Boer sounded surly. "Them?" he said thickly, "In there."

There was a pause. Then rapid footsteps approaching. Bolts slammed back until they clanged in their sockets. The door flung open. And by the meagre light of our candle-end we saw on the threshold a small, fierce, swarthy man, in glasses.

He surveyed the interior of the shed. We stared back, already fuddled with drink. Then I saw for the first time that characteristic flame-like flicker of intense emotions in his face: disgust, distress, compassion, outrage.

"Why are these men chained?"

The Boer was behind him now, with the lantern. "It is the custom, monsieur. They run, otherwise." He shrugged. "You lose money."

That remark was a mistake. The agent turned on him a look of such scorching contempt that the Boer backed a step. He was twice the agent's weight, and taller by a full handspan – and yet he flinched.

"Unlock them. All of them. Now."

"Monsieur, I assure you, it is necessary."

"No. Nowhere else in the islands is it necessary. It is not necessary here."

He watched, scowling savagely, as the Boer sullenly unlocked each shackle. The candle-end began to burn out.

"You have another lantern?"

The man nodded.

"Then leave this one here."

Again, the fool began to protest, "Monsieur, there is drinking, fighting, the danger of fire . . ."

"*Leave it.*"

When they had gone, the babble broke out.

"Two days," Matthieu declared. "That's all I give him."

Most of us agreed. The Boer would get rid of him somehow. An accident, a fall, snakebite – we felt no compunction.

We underestimated him. Next morning, the overseer was gone. Dismissed. We heard Monsieur giving orders for the house to be cleaned. He had a fine voice, I remember thinking, and a fine flow of language. An educated man. He reminded him a little of Père Martin, whose pupil I had once been, a lifetime ago.

That day the gangs worked unchained. All day Monsieur patrolled the fields on horseback – saying nothing, giving no orders and yet ubiquitous, always within sight. He watched us under drawn brows, with his habitual scowling glare. We noted the rifle he carried, and exchanged our own, apprehensive glances. Yet when he did fire – a shocking, heart-stopping noise in the murmuring quiet – it was not on a runaway, but on a buck drinking at a waterhole. He slung it behind his saddle. We did not learn until later that the meat was destined for our supper as well as his own.

Severe he looked – but when old Matthieu stumbled and cut his foot on Denis's machete he was there in seconds. He had bandages; he staunched the bleeding, bound the wound, cut a stout cane as a crutch and sent Matthieu limping back to the compound to rest.

Matthieu was so astonished he protested. "Monsieur, I can still work."

"No. The wound must be kept clean, or it will suppurate."

In the afternoon he said abruptly, "Do you commonly work in silence like this? Do you never talk amongst yourselves, or sing?"

I said, "We do both, m'sieur. But . . ."

The eyebrows lifted and the long mouth twitched. "But my presence inhibits you. Yes. Then forget that I am here. I am observing today, and learning. Nothing more. Sing if you wish."

We interpreted that as a command. Antoine began a chorus. It was ragged at first, self-consciously diffident – but it gave rhythm to the work and soon we were all singing. He rode amongst us and for the first time I saw him smile.

Back in the compound he made a florid gesture of dismissal. "Go. Do whatever you wish before dinner." And he strode off, whistling, to the house which had been the Boer's, and was now his.

Minutes later we heard a startled shout from within, a heavy thump and a fluent, prolonged oath.

It should have been comic – but no-one laughed. Instead, we stared at one another in sudden comprehension, and something like dismay.

"Céline!" Denis said.

I ran – a number of us ran. We surged up the steps and onto the verandah without a thought of trespass or what the penalty might be – ran as though we cared what happened to this small angry man.

At the threshold, resolution failed. We crowded, but none of us entered.

The snake lay on the heap of linen which had concealed it within his trunk and which he had evidently just lifted and tossed onto his bed. How he had escaped being bitten was a mystery.

He looked up, but seemed not to see us. His jaw was set hard. He strode to the doorway and we moved aside to let him through. He did not speak. He descended the steps, crossed the yard. The snake could have been captured now, but no-one moved: we were all watching him. He selected a pitchfork from the stack, one with narrow tines, very sharp. As he returned we parted like a black sea to give him passage.

He stood over the snake, his expression thoughtful, calculating, the pitchfork grasped tines-down in his right hand. His left hand moved in front of the reptile's head. It lunged and gaped for the strike. The pitchfork came down lightning-fast, piercing through shirts, drawers, cravats, pantaloons, sheets, mattress and all – and the stretched neck was pinned just behind the head. He reached down and grasped the snake at the point where the jaw angles into the neck. As he drew it out unharmed from under the pitchfork, it thrashed violently, and coiled its thick heavy length around his forearm.

Still he said nothing. And apart from a collective sigh when the reptile was finally captured, neither did we.

He approached the door again, carrying his deadly trophy. We moved hastily aside. By now every man, woman and child in the compound had gathered close around the verandah; retreat could have become a rout had he chosen to use his captive as a weapon of retaliation.

He did not. He stood there against the railing, looking down on the sea of upturned black faces. No-one moved. Then astonishingly, the eyes began to dance, the mouth curled into a rueful self-deprecatory grin. He made a helpless shrugging gesture and pointed to the snake, indicating the ludicrous dilemma he now found himself in: he did not know how to let go. In a voice shaking with mirth he demanded, "So – what should I do now?"

And suddenly we were all laughing at him and with him. The humour was irresistible. We couldn't stop ourselves. The women shrieked, the men howled and hooted. Feet stamped, bellies were clutched, tears streamed helplessly down dusty faces.

Céline walked up to him. Even her grim face betrayed the ghost of a smile. She gripped the reptile by the tail, unwrapped the coils, captured the head, and threw it into the stand of elephant grass behind the house.

Monsieur bowed, and shook her hand with solemn courtesy.

"Tell me, madame," he inquired, "Should I expect any more surprises of that nature tonight?"

Céline, equally grave, equally courteous, replied "No, monsieur."

I became aware that he was looking thoughtfully at me.

"You are Joseph", he said. "Joseph Gautier."

I bowed, trying to conceal my apprehension. "Yes, m'sieur."

"Père Martin tells me you are literate. Numerate, also."

I said, "M'sieur, I can read and write and compute after a fashion, but I am not learned."

An intent piercing look from under the eyebrows. Then an abrupt, satisfied nod.

"Come to see me early tomorrow. There are matters I wish to discuss."

"Monsieur, tomorrow I must cut the cane."

"No. Tomorrow you consult with me."

All of this I remembered as I escorted his woman to the house that had been his. It was not large. Wooden, supported on coconut stumps; one long many-windowed room within, the wide verandah surrounding it, the sleeping-room at the back.

She paused at the threshold, and I heard her breath catch in her throat.

"You have kept it exactly as it was?"

I nodded.

"All his books . . . his belongings . . ."

"As best we could, mademoiselle. In this climate, it is not easy . . . paper swells, becomes discoloured, fabric rots . . ."

"Yes. I see."

She moved slowly across the room, to his desk. She lowered herself almost fearfully into his chair. Touched the bundle of quills, the penknife, held his journal for a moment between her palms.

"It is as though he never left. As though he . . ."

Her face contracted. "May I be alone here for a little while?"

A few minutes later I heard her weeping.

Early, he had said. At six-thirty, when I knocked, he was at his desk writing, having washed, shaved, dressed and breakfasted.

He bade me sit, which I did with some reluctance. He began, I remember, by interrogating me as to the extent of my education. He was not satisfied – I learnt later that in matters of scholarship he was never satisfied – and yet, when the ordeal was over the penetrating scowl relaxed and he looked at me with something approaching approval.

"Is there anyone else who can read and write amongst you?"

"No-one, monsieur."

"No other leaders in your community? Those respected amongst you? Women also, not only men?"

I shook my head. "Only Céline, monsieur, and she . . ."

"Then fetch her."

I hesitated. "Monsieur, Céline is . . ."

He waited, eyebrows raised. It was hard to continue. "Céline is *obeah*, monsieur. The obeah-woman. You have heard of this?"

He nodded. A flicker of distaste across his face, hardening into resolve. "Then she is respected. Perhaps feared. All the more reason for us to gain her support."

"Us," he had said, as though I was already an ally. As I went off in search of Céline I wondered if this was indeed so. Was I on his side? And if so, against whom? or what?

What he discussed with us that morning was nothing less than the ending of the only world Céline and I had ever known.

"There *will* be abolition," he said. "And this time the law will not be repealed. I find it shameful that France has lagged so far behind England in this matter. But the English abolition was badly managed, it created severe hardship. Here we have the opportunity to prepare ourselves adequately."

Ourselves. As though we were social equals, sharing the same predicament. Céline and I exchanged bemused glances.

"I have two tasks to perform here," he went on. "One is to satisfy my employers: to revive this wasted estate and make it profitably. The other is to prepare you all for freedom. I see no grounds for conflict between the two."

He turned to Céline. "Madame – this house: would you say it was suitable for the climate and the conditions here at La Carène?"

She raised an eyebrow. "Is Monsieur proposing to move the workers into the house and remove himself to the shed?"

He appreciated her quickness, and laughed. "No. But houses like this must be built. A house for each family. Each family with a garden to support itself if needful. Freedom can be as harsh as slavery, madame."

There were many problems. Fifteen years of brutal dehumanisation cannot be reversed overnight, however sincere the goodwill. He was not a patient man, and sometimes his exacerbated nerves drove him to an explosion of fury. He would retreat into his garden then and dig – stripped to the waist in the scorching sun, digging and digging until the temper eased. Afterwards, he would be contrite: "What did I say? I cannot remember." But by then we loved him. His faults only endeared him to us the more.

The most violent quarrels concerned the allocation of the new homes being built. There were no families as he understood the term. Men and women had bedded indiscriminately – and neither could cope with the new situation. There were riots, and two murders.

It was Céline who suggested the solution – one which rather shocked him.

"Let the houses be built by all, as we agreed," she said, "But give them to the women. Let the women decide which men shall share with them."

He did not like it, but pragmatist that he was, he acceded.

After half an hour she came out on to the verandah, and called me. She was weary, but composed.

"Will you show me his garden?"

He had loved his garden. He had created it; it was his private retreat. As we walked the sun-latticed paths I named the plants for her: frangipani, hibiscus, papaya, bougainvillea, allamanda, star-fruit and passion-vine. Here he had read her letters, which came by almost every boat. Here he had written his to her, on the long bench under the jacaranda tree.

He had received other letters too – from a cousin of his, who had a financial interest in this place (which he did not). The import was always the same: the estate was not showing enough profit.

"Not enough profit? For God's sake – the profit has trebled since I arrived. What does she want – my bones, my flesh, my blood? *Our* blood?"

Once she mentioned his woman. In that letter she had proposed retaining him here for a fourth year. He was angry enough to show it to me.

"After all, cousin, a year is nothing, I am sure you are anxious to return to your cold disdainful Miss Snowe, but I beg you to consider the attractions of another year of freedom before taking that passionless icicle to your bosom for life."

It was not my place to comment. But my face must have shown my surprise: he was a passionate man.

"She was orphaned young," he explained softly. "Unloved, unwanted, her few outward deficiencies ridiculed, her natural feelings suppressed . . . When I first knew her she was full of self-distrust. An onlooker at life, passive as a shadow. Deeply unhappy."

Yet he loved her, and no other. She was constantly in his thoughts. And now, walking beside her in the garden he had made, I began to understand why.

I had asked him, "Will you stay?"

He had sighed. "I am torn, my friend."

"Could she not come here?"

He relit his cigar. "It begins to be possible now. I must return home in the autumn. Then, we shall see."

But when the time came his ship sailed without him. He had contracted fever. A fortnight later he was dead.

All of this – and more than I had intended – I told her as we walked in his garden. Unlike him, she had the gift of silence.

"I know you so well, through his letters," she said quietly. "You were his friend. I doubt if he ever had a closer and truer friend than you."

She looked up at the blue-grey peaks, the precipitous forests, the glittering sea.

"It is so beautiful. I did not believe any place on earth could be so lovely."

"He wanted you to see it," I said.

She smiled. "The Delectable Mountains . . . Emmanuel's Land."

I looked puzzled, and she laughed. "You are a good Catholic, as he was. You do not know the Pilgrim's Progress?"

"No."

"I am glad I came," she added. "I was not sure – but . . . Now I see what he saw. And he . . . he is still here, somehow. I can feel it."

Towards sundown the whole village accompanied her to his grave. I had had misgivings, but when we arrived the grave was Christian, decent, heaped with fresh flowers.

It was an ordeal, but a necessary one, and she bore it bravely. She knelt briefly at the headstone, with its inscription – Paul Carl David Emmanuel, and the date. I offered her a bunch of frangipani, but she refused. "I never give flowers to those I love," she said. Instead she placed a thin gold chain on the grave, unclasped from around her neck.

She spent much of the next day alone. But in the evening she sent for me.

"I shall leave tomorrow," she said. "My presence here is an embarrassment, I know."

I felt a stab of regret. But she was right. "Should I fetch Père Martin to escort you?"

"No." An impish, conspiratorial glance. "Maurice will contrive, as he did before." So Maurice, too had fallen under the spell of this slight woman with the shadowed, luminous smile.

"His possessions – will you take them with you?"

"Would it grieve you to lose them?"

I nodded. "But they are yours, mademoiselle."

"No. I have no right to anything that was his. I was not his wife, you see. I am merely the woman that he might have married one day, had he lived."

I was angry. "You were far more than that to him. He loved no-one but you."

A brief, hitching sigh. "Perhaps."

The moon had risen. Cicadas rasped in the nearby bushes. I wanted to stir, to light the lamp, to break this mood of intimacy which had come upon us. But she sat pale as the moonlight, as still and as thoughtful, and I sat as though tranced, watching her.

"It is so much his room," she said softly. "One feels his presence everywhere, but here it is so strong . . . as though he has just left for a moment . . ."

I nodded. "I sit here sometimes, in the evenings. Not in his chair, of course, that would not be seemly. But here, where I always sat. And sometimes I believe I can smell his cigar, hear his step outside the verandah . . ."

"Rapid, regular, intent . . ."

"The door bursting open before him, clashing behind . . ."

"That frowning glare of his . . ."

"Melting instantly into that smile . . ."

The image we had conjured was so vivid I turned, half-believing it to be real. *Obeah*, I thought – and terror sent a rush of coldness into my belly. For there *was* a presence in that room; a force so vital and so vigorous it set my blood racing and brought both of us to our feet. In my confusion I even thought I smelt cigar smoke.

She was trembling violently. Her eyes were dark with unshed tears.

"How can I leave this place?" she whispered. "How can I leave *him*?"

We moved towards each other involuntarily, she to seek comfort, I – God knows what I sought. She was close enough for me to smell her white woman's scent and a faint sweet odour of flowers.

What she saw I do not know. A black man, taller than her lover, gaunt, work-hardened, greying prematurely at the temples . . . or something, someone else.

"Joseph," she said, bewildered as a child. "Paul . . ."

I stood there, immobile, heart pounding in my chest, vision blurred, hardly able to breathe, fire in my veins, knowing that what I desired meant certain death: a horrible, public death by flogging, if poison failed to forestall.

My hand moved independent of my will, as though guided by a consciousness which was not mine. I watched it with amazement. It touched her hair, that soft, straight pale hair slipping through the fingers like strands of silk, cool on the surface, warm at the scalp. The fingers stroked her cheek, feeling there the slight roughness of scars I had scarcely noticed until now. They tilted her chin upwards – and again without conscious exercise of will I bent and kissed her lips.

I felt her hands tighten on my shoulders, her whole body shudder and respond. My scruples vanished – all higher and meaner thoughts evaporated like water spilt in the sun. I kissed the sweet hollow at the base of her throat, and as I loosened the braided coil of her hair she gave a sharp soft intake of breath, as though the action was familiar, and dear to her. Then force flowed through me, passion infused with a powerful gentleness I have never experienced before.

Was he indeed with us there, in that shadowed room with the moonlight latticed across the bare board floor? Was I the channel for a ghostly revenant's love? Was this his last gift to her, and to me? – his final farewell? I do not know.

She felt it too. "Joseph," she breathed as I lifted her in my arms, and then, a little later, "*Paul* . . ."

We made love slowly, sweetly, powerfully. At the end her face was wet with tears, but her eyes were shining.

"He loves me," she said, "he does love me."

Then, for a long while, we loved each other.

When I awoke, she had gone.

I went to the kitchen. "Where is mademoiselle?"

Céline shrugged. "She left before dawn, with Maurice."

"I heard nothing," I said.

She nodded. "Better so."

And she was right. What could we have said to one another? What promises could we have made? Where on this earth could we be together? Better a clean departure, however intense the regret.

Céline said abruptly, "I gave her a *bonne-maman*."

Abortifacient. My breath caught in my throat.

Whether she used it – or had occasion to use it – I do not know.

A long time later, I heard a scrap of gossip concerning a white woman who had taught for almost a year at a mission school in Martinique. She had given her name as Madame Gautier and told them she was recently widowed. She was pregnant.

Perhaps it was she. Perhaps not.

By the time the news reached me, she and her infant daughter had departed for France.

I should like to see my daughter one day. But it would not altogether surprise me if she were to resemble him rather than me.

AMANDA METCALFE

# re: Fragments Discovered on Hill No. 406/22a

**I enclose the papers recovered from the area of the witnessed aerial abduction of Mrs. M. Fleury last week. I look forward to your comments.**

P. Devereux (Col.)

## FRAGMENT ONE

Why do I have to suffer this and still think what to cook for dinner? That's one thing you didn't have to do. Isn't it.

Although according to you that's the only difference and according to you I'm not doing so great. You didn't spend your time like me howling for death but shouldered your "burden" and got on with it. Further, I'm to stop calling you a bloody torturer because you're only implementing my idea which you warned me at the time would be too much but I insisted. You say you have control over what I do but not how I do it. If I could stop crying for a moment I could see that. Every single thing you've sent me I've resisted. You've found me reluctant to shoulder anything never mind my "burden" which you say isn't so hard, and I've been given much in my visions and that four days of ecstasy. (Did you have this? Or not? You say it's the same but it's so hard to know what's real). As for pride that I've done it, I should forget it because you've had to drag me through it screaming and kicking and it's been horrible for you. Could I not have some thought for someone else besides myself.

Then you said you might think about making another Rose, a red one this time, stronger than white, red for love. White is weak and cold. Red is warm and alive. Perhaps she would have long brown hair and sparkling eyes like yours, and perhaps also make a better fist of all this than I have done. Although almost anyone would., wouldn't they. "Don't you see," you said, "how people will never believe a feeble specimen like you who is so privileged and idle yet who does nothing but whine and complain and beg for death?"

Then suddenly you said, "Rose, you're perfect, please don't worry," and then, "Why did you say that, stop talking to yourself and pretending it's me. Perfect don't make me laugh" and so on. This new Rose would be fit to have your child.

I was in Waitrose and I nearly doubled over with pain. I was buying some smoked salmon. "Oh very nice," you said, "what about people who can't afford it. You're so spoiled. And I'm only telling you the truth, like you wanted me to."

It wasn't as bad as Black Thursday when that terrible creature told me you didn't exist. Nothing could be as bad as that. If you don't exist – but that is unthinkable. Unthinkable.

I walked up the hill with difficulty, the bags from Waitrose banging against my legs. Michael says I'm weak because I'm so thin, and if only I'd eat more I'd feel better but it isn't that. It's you. It's you. You've made me go mad with your visions and your poetry and your rapture and your torture and your LIES. You knew I'd fall in love with you and I did. You knew you'd just have to show your face and I'd fall to bits and I did. But I thought you were love and it would be alright. It isn't alright. It's far from alright. You warned me of suffering, yes, and yes, I said that it would be okay. I could not think of anything worse than being without you. I could not think of this.

**FRAGMENT TWO**

. . . thing I did after my bath was to eat and drink my bread and water. I sat on the floor for a while, with my eyes closed, then I got up and went downstairs for some breakfast. I ate some toast in the kitchen, looking out at the garden. I thought about the bread and water. I felt no uncertainty about it. I felt no uncertainty then and I never have since. In all my doubting and all my anxiety, my trust in this food has remained inviolate. Naturally I've wondered why this is, and how it was that, on that late summer evening at

Tuesley, the pitta bread and the water was my eucharist. Had God, in the face of Peter's triple denial, simply stepped in and ordained me himself? Or was it that we are, each one, automatically ordained when love has entirely possessed us?

**FRAGMENT THREE**

. . . down my pen. I stared at the words on the page, not daring to confront the idea which had come to rest, very gently, in my mind. I said, "This can't be true. You can't mean it."

"It is true. And I do mean it."

I took up my pen again, and I wrote, very slowly, "Jesus began to write. He wrote a book."

He wrote a book –

"Which still exists."

"Which still – which WHAT?"

"Which still exists, Rose."

Still staring at the page I stood up. Then I sat down again. Then I walked round the room. I sat on the bed. I lay on the floor with my fist in my mouth. I went out onto the balcony, my fingers pressed to my temples. "Which still exists." I went into the bathroom. I came out again and poured myself a large brandy.

"Not too much, we have a long way to go tonight, and much to do."

"It's medicinal. I won't be going anywhere or doing anything without it."

I went back to my desk. "Alright," I said. "I'm ready. Where is it and let's go get it."

The reply was a long story – confusing, mixed, sometimes allegorical sometimes literal. Sometimes it made sense and sometimes it didn't. There was something about Brussels, something about a death camp, something about a bank vault which might have been in Brussels or might have been in Basel. There was something hideously frightening; something – oh, excruciatingly sad. A child, a secret password, a dreadful betrayal, a fountain, a garden, someone running through rainy darkness. A terrified pregnant woman, a widow, a Jew. Great loss, the need for secrecy, obscured identity. Papers burned, papers scattered, fragments on a dry hillside – Egypt? Israel? France? Greece?

Then no, the identity wasn't exactly obscured. It was and it wasn't. There's a lie in here somewhere. A church, a betrayal. Jesus? Was it Jesus? He didn't exist! No and yes. His name was not Jesus but John. John took the story of the crucified Zealot and – I can't HEAR this properly, what are you SAYING?

The book is hidden, the identities changed. It is in a cave, a bank vault, scattered, burned, unrecognised. Someone has it, part of it. A collector. He does not know what it is . . .

**FRAGMENT FOUR**

I love you. I love you with all my mind and with all my heart and with all my spirit and with all my body. I love you with every fibre and bone and bit of tissue. Every shard of my being is pierced by love for you.

You say you are coming. In a spaceship, to take me home. Like Jesus, or John, or whatever his name was. As it was for you so will it be for me. An ascension, no less. How can I believe this? And, loving you so much, how can I not believe it? Was there ever such a torment of doubt. Yes there was. It was yours. Before you – before the – before you were lifted up. It was yours. You've been here, you've known this. I am not the first to suffer these things.

**FRAGMENT FIVE**

. . . returned to the hotel I was not howling nor shrieking nor cursing with pain but whispering with it. I whispered to you that I did not want to hear your voice or your instructions ever again. I did not intend to write another word, another syllable, for you and if I did I would burn it immediately. I was going to go down to the sea and to throw all the notebooks into it, and watch them drown one by one as I have not the courage to drown myself.

After you did not arrive at the church I walked through the cemetery to the end where there is a steep gorge, drop of hundreds of feet. A fall from there would almost certainly kill. I do not know why I did not jump. The pain was certainly bad enough. It was beyond words, beyond any kind of sound, or mark one may make on a piece of paper. Every nerve ending was exposed and screaming with pain. This is what love does. It is not possible to communicate how it feels. Only those who have experienced it themselves will know.

I reached the hotel cold and wet for it's pouring again and feels more like Liverpool than the Côte d'Azur. I had a hot bath. I told you quietly to go away and preferably kill yourself. Or at least leave me alone. I do not know who you are, but whoever you are you are plainly mad. Also have nothing to do with love. If indeed you have ever heard of it.

There were no more pictures, visions. I could not see you, I could not see baby Rose. As for all that tripe with the spaceship, that had certainly gone. All manner of violence was going on in my head in word and deed, but I do not know who was doing what to whom because I too have gone mad and cannot any longer recognise my own voice.

I thought about Jesus, sorry, John, about what happened to him poor bugger. Got caught with the same line I did. He did not ascend. When they open the cave they will find not only the book but also a pile of bones. Already half dead with grief and repeated betrayals he walled himself up and starved himself. Or maybe died of anguish. I don't know. But he didn't ascend.

What happened was he went out on that wretched mountain with his friends, having told them he was going to ascend into heaven and that they should come and watch. So they did. A cloud then came and separated them. No-one could see anything at all, never mind an ascension. When Jesus – oh sod it JOHN – realised that nothing was going to happen he was so humiliated that he ducked down behind some rocks and hid from them. They then all thought that he had gone to heaven in the cloud because they were all very stupid and gullible, just like me.

I remembered – too late – Black Thursday and the creature

explaining that there was no beautiful man and no babies. That heaven was incomprehensible to such as me. It was abstract. Bliss, but abstract. "What nonsense," it had said. "How could a man, a physical man, be assumed into an abstraction!"

Search me, I thought. Bloody search me.

Towards evening I calmed down a bit. I had a short sleep and wrote a bit more about the cave, the book, the pile of bones. Then I became depressed again and wrote that I didn't think I was God after all. Nothing fantastic was going to happen to me. I was going to have to carry on living with this dreadful pain for a natural span. Then I would just conk out like everyone else. Why should I be any different.

Then I began to wonder if God existed at all. What was the evidence? None. Who was writing in my notebooks? Me. Who had given myself all this junk to write? I had.

I went back to the very beginning. Did I believe in the creation or was it just an accident? And so on. I realised that I had no idea what I believed at all. I had become so detached and so abstracted that I could not really make myself believe that I was alive, or that there was a world of real things in which I lived.

As for God, I really couldn't say. My sense of perspective, my instinct for what was loopy and what was not, had completely disappeared. It may be said that it had disappeared long since, and that may be so, but I hadn't noticed it. I felt cut adrift. Did Eze exist? Where was Richmond? Anywhere near Nazareth? How had I arrived here? By train? Or by spaceship? How old was I? Thirty-eight? Or a zillion trillion billion? Had I been born? Or had I come by osmosis? What was my name? Did I have one? Was it Rose? Jesus? Maid Marion?

I wrote myself into yet another stupor. I note from my journals that I was still writing at 2.45am. I can't bring myself to read what I wrote. It's almost illegible anyway. I think that I went to bed around 3.30am.

I know that I slept.

**FRAGMENT SIX**

. . . hospital. They stuck needles in me and gave me pills which made me not know who I was any more. Before they drugged me they asked me who the prime minister was. Smiling, I told them. They showed me a wristwatch and asked me what it was. Again smiling I described it. John Major! A wristwatch! Yes I have plenty of friends but yes I also like solitude. No I never wanted children, and neither did Michael. Today is Wednesday, Wednesday 30 October. The time is seven in the evening. I am here because my husband thinks I'm barmy. I do not want your pills but I will take them if you promise me that I will not lose my clarity.

"The pills will give you clarity, Mrs Fleury. That is what they are for."

A plastic cup with coloured capsules. I swallowed them watched by a friendly nurse in a blue dress. The next morning I could barely remember my own name, never mind the prime minister's. I may have recognised a wristwatch. I don't know.

The psychiatrist, most eminent, took Michael into his opulent office. The one with the long windows swathed in peach damask and the lichen coloured carpet. Choice pieces of antique walnut furniture and a desk the size of this room.

"We believe your wife may be suffering from schizophrenia." Michael could not speak. The death knell. The impossible word, the eternal word with no cure.

"We can probably control it, if indeed that is what it is. But your wife will be medicated for the rest of her life."

Michael went home and sat alone in the dark. He could not tell anyone. After a while he put his head in his hands. I would have wept for him as I weep for him now, but I did not know. Nobody told me, not until much later. The death knell. The impossible, the endless word.

Everything except you became blurred and incomprehensible. But you I heard. "There was no resurrection, I did not die," then, "I was not even crucified." A mistake? No, a metaphor. It was all a metaphor. I told you in Eze, it was based on someone else's life. Jesus the Zealot, a brave man, killed for his beliefs; a wise man, of whom many were jealous. But the narrative was not literal. It was an allegory. A divine allegory. I listened in silence. At least I was not crying anymore. "There is but one Rose," you said gently, "Your sickness manufactured the others. And I was never angry with You. How could I be? I love you more than life, more than death."

The psychiatrist arrived with a young woman, his registrar. She had a notebook. They sat down by my bed.

"And have you been hearing from God lately?"

"I – I don't know. It sounds crazy when you say it like that."

"Whatever. Have you heard him?"

"I guess."

"And what has he been saying?"

"It sounds mad."

"Never mind. We have to discuss this things. What has be been saying?"

"There was no resurrection, he did not die."

The registrar wrote in her notebook.

"Anything else?"

"Isn't that enough?"

"Did he say anything else?"

"He was not crucified."

"Have you been eating properly?"

"I eat what I'm given. But –"

"Sleeping?"

"All the time."

"And this is the extent of the communications?"

I hesitated.

"Well?"

"He's going to come and get me," I said, "When all this is over. He'll come in a spaceship, and I'll go home with him." The registrar looked up. "Who?" she said, "Who will come and get you?"

"I cannot say it."

"Do you mean God? God will come and get you?"

"Sort of."

"Yes or no."

"Yes."

"We're going to increase your medication," the psychiatrist intervened crisply. "The side effects will be lessened if you put on a little weight. Do you think you could do that?"

"I don't know. I eat what I'm given. But –"

"Then we shall have to give you a little more." He stood, businesslike, smiling. He shook my hand. "We are making progress," he said, "You may not notice it but we do. You are getting better. But you must try to be calm, try not to resist us. Rest. The medicine will help if you'll allow it. Believe me."

You were still telling me I was to die. I didn't understand then as I understand now. I did not understand that it was an inner death. I thought it was external, materially real. "At Christmas," you said, but not which one. I was not afraid. It was what I wanted. I could not see how I could live with the pain of this love so far from its object. And no-one would ever believe what I said, about anything, especially not now I was schizophrenic. The seriously mad are always unheard. I was seriously mad. I knew that I might just as well be dead.

**FRAGMENT SEVEN**

It all got too much for Michael and he left. There was a woman, young of course, met her at work. She made him laugh, she was interested in his life. I felt grateful to her. She did not sound like someone who would turn crazy on him. She did not sound like someone who would start believing she was God.

But, all the same, when Michael left I felt – oh, so lonely. Desperately lonely. I wrote the book to fight it off. But it didn't really work. I could not make myself want to live.

**FRAGMENT EIGHT**

[This section has suffered from considerable heat damage and we've been able to piece together only very small segments. However, I include it as it is clearly part of the main text, P.D.]

. . . I do remember, with all too vivid clarity, was the terror which descended on me after the first application of ECT. Far from being unafraid I was now terror-stricken. I was absolutely certain that I would indeed lapse into that coma under one of the anaesthetics, but that the coma would be so deep and so penetrative that it would be mistaken for death. I would then be buried alive.

. . . remember is sight, sound, vision . . . I can remember holding tightly to the nurse's hand, saying "Please don't let go of me. Please don't." And her saying, "I'll still be holding on when you wake up. Don't be afraid. Nothing is going to happen to" . . . alarm clock sounding in the dark morning . . . lurid orange lights in the bus which . . . nightmarish.

. . . of the hospital, the smell of ashtrays in the waiting room . . . sound of my footsteps, echoing in the dark and empty street.

. . . terror was absolute. I cannot imagine . . . constant companion. But never more so. Never more so.

Christmas came and went and was . . . my cousin Tim who electrocuted . . . killed himself . . . obsessed with the fact that . . . he was not dead. I wrote about it on . . . brink of a nervous breakdown . . .suffered the same trauma as his. Locked . . . unable to move or . . . breathe . . . paralysed unto death but to still be conscious? Is . . . before . . . buried or . . . alive. It is the . . . horrific nightmare anyone can . . . worse than a nightmare. It is real.

**FRAGMENT NINE**

Somehow we found ourselves in the Church of the Holy Sepulchre. It was late in the afternoon, we were the only ones there. And then suddenly I was standing before the entrance to the so-called tomb. I bent down and went inside. There was a slab of rose marble, some candles, a painting. There was complete silence. The strange thing was that it did not feel bogus. I could easily imagine how a believer would be overwhelmed in this place by an apparency of truth. In fact it was quite difficult to believe that this was not where a great miracle had occurred. There was not a trace of manufacture. I realised at that moment how crucial it had been that I had not visited Jerusalem before. If I had done so, before the verity of what God had told me was scored into my soul, I would have defected in a moment.

For two or three days we dawdled in the city. We went to the Western Wall, bought glossy black olives, hommous, richly coloured vegetables in the souk, slept in the heat of the afternoons, rested in cafés, drank the repulsive local wine and cooked long languorous meals in the evenings. I began at last to be aware, indeed as one dragged from the grave, of life.

On the fourth day we walked the Via Dolorosa. On the steps in the Moslem Quarter a kid or a lamb had just been slaughtered and the blood was being hosed away. The carcass lay split wide on the shiny stones, its guts spilling around it. I thought immediately of John and of his allegory. We stepped carefully around the victim. Lamb of God, animate metaphor, sacrificed on the steps of the Holy City.

I was profoundly in awe of John's literary brilliance. The more of his sources I discovered – in Greek mythology, in the Old Testament, in old legends of ancient Sumer, Egypt, Mesopotamia – and the more clearly I could see the way he had stitched them into images of his own experience, the more in awe of him I became. Only God could be so adroit. Only God could be so multidimensionally clever. Only God could mean everything in a word.

On the fifth day we drove to En-Gedi, having hired a car from the fabulously rude staff at the Herz office. We drove through the Arab settlements a little nervously – we'd watched *Newsnight* a few times before we'd left the UK – but met with nothing more than mild curiosity. At a tatty checkpoint a tired looking soldier waved us through.

And then the desert. Pale silky hills unfolded before us under a white sky. Then the dry hot fierce mountains along the perimeter of the Dead Sea. I fell instantly in love with it.

At En-Gedi it was violently hot. I went to my room at the Field Study Centre and slept immediately. Nick went to swim in the famous salt sea.

The next morning, early, we set out for the cave. I knew roughly where it was, it was marked on the map as the Lovers' Cave, in the Nahal David Nature Reserve.

It was a long climb in direct sunlight with temperatures well over a hundred. The pale gold rocks were baking and the path was extremely steep.

After about two hours we came suddenly to a spring. There was vegetation, several linked turquoise pools, softly rounded honey rocks, the infinitely refreshing sound of rushing water. Without hesitation we plunged in. During this bliss my dwindling intellect disappeared altogether. There was nothing left but body and dreams. Afterwards we sat in the shade of the rocks and ate smoked cheese, bread, olives, tomatoes, hommous, dates and yoghurt. It was clear that we were in Paradise.

The cave was exactly as I had seen it in my visions. Above a pool and beside a waterfall. I didn't have the strength to climb up to it but Nick did. I knew, of course, that it would be blocked, and it was. "Stalactites," Nick called down, "Completely solid."

Not a rockfall, then, as I had supposed. I shouted back above the din of the water, "How long would they take to form?" He came back to the lip of the cave. "I don't know – hundreds of years, maybe more. Shall I come down now or shall I give you a hand up?"

"No I wouldn't make it, it's too steep."

I watched him climb down.

"So it would or could have been open two thousand years ago?"

"I would think almost certainly."

We stood in chest deep water. We looked at each other.

"That's where he was," I said. "That's where I saw him."

"It certainly matches your description."

The tomb of the chrysalis. The place where John died and was buried. The place where God was born. Place of joy and of sorrow, hinged to the dying and rising gods of religion's cradle. Inner death, inner burial, inner birth, fed by the baptismal fountain, nurtured by the beloved.

**FRAGMENT TEN**

"A pink star."

"Pink?"

"Must I repeat everything?"

"I'm just trying to be clear, that's all."

"It would look pink anyway, from where you are."

"It's where you live?"

"Not exactly. It's a kind of navigational aid."

"Crikey."

"You do have a way with words, Rose."

I looked for pink stars in an astronomy book at Waterstone's. There weren't any. There were red stars, Antares, Betelgeuse, Cephei, Aldebaran, but no pink ones. Then I read another book, about alien abductions. I became depressed. "This doesn't sound anything like you," I said. "These people have been kidnapped by little grey items who've done vile things to their insides aboard spaceships. What's it got to do with us?"

"Nothing."

"But there's kind of, well, evidence. They come back with inexplicable wounds and scars. I don't understand. I don't like it."

"Don't be afraid. Nothing will ever harm you."

"But you are going to come for me?"

"Oh yes."

"Soon?"

"When you are ready."

"I'm ready now. In fact definitely now. Before my next gas bill arrives."

"You don't believe me, but it will happen."

"Forgive me. But I can't let myself. Look what happened in Eze. I can't go through that again."

"You won't have to."

[This concludes the documentation collected at the site. I append the witness statements to give you some idea of what they seem to think happened. P.D.]

**STATEMENT ONE**

Name:
Jean-Antoine Pin.
Occupation:
Camp Site Manager.
Age: 34

"It was an overcast night, quite windy, you could see the full moon now and then through the clouds. I was just doing my rounds and I suddenly heard a loud humming sound coming from the east side of the camp. I went to investigate, of course. The humming sound got louder and became almost deafening. When I got over there I saw a lot of lights in the sky, very high up. The clouds cleared, and then you could see this bloody great thing looked like an airborne city. Some kind of small craft came out of it – moving quite slowly. Bit like a helicopter. It came and hovered about thirty, maybe forty, metres above the woman. Then she just kind of floated up into it, with her suitcase and everything. If I'd been on my own, I'd have thought I was dreaming. But I couldn't have been dreaming, because other people were there, and they saw it, too. We all saw it."

**STATEMENT TWO**

Name:
Gedalia Ha'am.
Occupation
Sales assistant.
Age: 19

"It was very still, no moon, but you could see a lot of stars. Suddenly this sort of saucer thing came zooming out of nowhere. It didn't make any noise, which was really the freakiest thing. It stopped suddenly and stayed about ten or so metres above the woman. Then a door or hatch opened, and a beam of white light came out of it. The woman walked into the light, and disappeared. Just like that. Here one minute, gone the next. The weirdest thing

I ever saw. Then the saucer thing zoomed away again, and that was that. There were some sheets of paper lying around, and I wondered if they had anything to do with it, so I picked them up and gave them to the colonel."

**STATEMENT THREE**

Name:
Penny Unwin.

Occupation:
Lay Preacher.

Age: 48

"My therapist has told me that collective hallucinations aren't uncommon. Like the Angel of Mons, for instance. People see what they want to see, and create their own metaphors. This spaceship we all think we saw is certainly a metaphor of some kind – we're still working on what it might mean. My pattern is that when I'm stressed I tend to use symbolism to distance myself from it. I'm very stressed just now, so it's obvious where all this spaceship stuff has come from. I'd like to forget about it, to be honest, but my therapist wants me to stay with the process, she says if I don't I'll never self-actualise or get at my personal truth."

**STATEMENT FOUR**

Name:
Matthias Ivge.

Occupation:
Cleaner.

Age: 23

"I couldn't sleep so I left my tent and went for a walk. I saw this woman standing by herself near the ruined church, like she was waiting for someone. Then this man appeared. I don't know where he came from. He was wearing a long white djellaba, like an Arab. He embraced her, and then they both like just de-materialised. She had a suitcase, and that went too. Hey it was weird. But it did happen. I saw it with my own eyes."

SHEENAGH PUGH

# Crossing the Bridge

He was on his way
to buy a wedding ring,
singing as he went.

Crossing Cardiff Bridge,
he met his old love,
and they fell in talk;

she wished him joy
of his wedding, and said
it was fine weather

for the time of year,
and his whole heart
went out to her.

Between water and air,
country and town,
the world alters:

*not here but there,*
*not Elizabeth but Joan,*
*not what I thought,*

*but what surprised me.*
He stood on a bridge
and let it happen,

or made it happen:
who knows how
these bridges work,

though we stand so often
on a stone moment,
an arc of choice,

or chance. Sometimes
we are Joan, the mover,
the change in the air;

sometimes the left-behind,
so much Elizabeth
under the bridge;

sometimes the man
in the middle, transfixed
by a shining word,

sun on his face,
the sweet certainty
that crossing the bridge

will change everything
for better or worse,
and he can't go back.

*Note* From an incident recounted by William Thomas in his *Diaries, 1762–1795*, pub. The Cardiff South Wales Record Society, 1995. Harry Edward went to buy the ring for his wedding to Elizabeth Water. Crossing the bridge into Cardiff, he met his old love Joan Morgan, and before he was over the bridge had decided to marry her instead, which he did.

JOHN GURNEY

# The Neutral Angel

Each time I come, your case seems slightly worse.
Cautiously I slip into your room,
on guard, expecting anything, rehearse
new words of cordial greeting. In the gloom
your eyes lurk in their corner, both on fire,
suspicious, as I offer them these gifts
to demonstrate my nature, my desire
to love you, and annul all former rifts
between us. Show the angel that I am
by Christmas cake, two pots of greengage jam.

The winter solstice darkens. It is three
and snowing very slightly. Small grey flakes
play anywhere. I sit down quietly,
take out my book and pencil, start to make
my usual notes. "It's for the Minister!"
I whisper, as I start to scribble down
the images around me, to transfer
old guilt to clean white paper. Now you frown.
'You've lost a lot of foliage!' you say.
'I know,' I murmur, in my casual way.

'It's serious!' you add, and once again
the forms I find around me start to preach.
Two crucifixes lean out from the chain
that bears the silver mirror. Out of reach,
three plates are hung. Black figures plan a fight.
Apollo reins four horses. Dark, severe,
Poseidon holds a trident. To his right
a militant Athene grips a spear.
Below, a small St. Joseph spends the hours
in contemplating shapes of paper flowers.

John Gurney

Your rigmarole begins. I note it all.
How Poisoners still slip beneath the door.
Can pass, as quick as X-rays, through the wall.
Are listening, from the centre of the floor.
Last night, you state, another boy was born.
The mother screamed for hours. All the staff
filed in to watch the murder. Cold, and worn,
I nod, write on in silence, never laugh,
a useless, neutral angel. Hell, I fear,
is terrible, repetitive, and here.

JONATHAN DAVIDSON

# The Sudden Shower

Time tells. The day clouds over.
A sudden shower. Rain beating a path
to our childhood door.

She is typing in the bedroom.
Broken notes. The bell's ping.
Her hand driving the bar back

to where its belongs again
and again until the rain's
persistent whisper sends us

flying up the garden path
to have wet washing stacked
on our arms, fist-fulls of pegs

stuffed in our pockets, always
the great haste to bring
the harvest home. What

she was typing is caught
half-in, half-out of being,
nearly naked. The clothes horse

is saddled-up, the gas fire
ticks and hisses, a dinner
is put in hand. We wait

for Dad's big soaking steps
to fill the kitchen, his voice
to clatter dishes. The poem's

not completed, gone already,
whisked along the gully,
swept down the storm drain.

AMANDA DALTON

# How to Disappear

First rehearse the easy things.
Lose your words in a high wind,
walk in the dark on an unlit road,
observe how other people mislay keys,
their diaries, new umbrellas.
See what it takes to go unnoticed
in a crowded room. Tell lies:
*I love you. I'll be back in half an hour.*
*I'm fine.*

Stand very still behind a tree,
become a cowboy, say you've died,
climb into wardrobes, breathe on a mirror
until there's no-one there, and practise magic,
tricks with smoke and fire –
a flick of the wrist and the victim's lost
his watch, his wife, his ten pound note. Perfect it.
Hold your breath a little longer every time.

Eat less, much less, and take a vow of silence.
Learn the point of vanishing, the moment
embers turned to ash, the sun fell down,
the sudden white-out came.
And when it comes again – it will –
just walk at it, walk into it, and walk,
until you know that you're no longer
anywhere.

JOHN GODFREY

# Time and Place

The map shows an old aerodrome a few
Miles to the north – that must have been the one –
And the shoreline's as he described it, so
Is the village. Is this quaint or what? His claim

That it all looked a little like New England
Is understandable: timber houses; small grey waves
Tripping over themselves; and the grating sound
Of shuffled shingle are all familiar. It gives

Her that craziest of ideas, the one of having been
Here before, as if knowledge of a place
Could be inherited. And standing in the lane
Outside the burned-out pub, she can share space,

Though not time, with a fresh-faced GI in his swank
New Officer's uniform and an adoring Suffolk girl,
Sees a brief slice of light and hears the clink
Of glasses and snatches of Glenn Miller that fall

out of the opening door. She watches the young couple
Leaving, arm in arm, and follows up the track
Past that tall, weird house. By the windmill
They light cigarettes, laugh as he tucks the pack

Into her coat-front, then gently make each other dumb
With kisses. From across The Meare half a dozen geese
Give raucous calls, strain into the air and climb
Ponderously, like overloaded bombers, heading east.

JOAN WILES

# Stephanotis

He like us to wear white.
Colour of skin no matter.
He say:
'White men full of virgin fantasies':
White stockings, white silk,
White petticoats and garters.

He like flowers in our hair.
Colour of hair no matter.
White 'n waxy blooms
Breathin' in their drug scent,
Their death scent, is like
A different kind of dyin'.

He like us to shake the rum.
Colour of rum no matter
So long as we pour cocktails
Long and slow,
Sing love songs in the afternoon,
Cast full-moon spells.

He like us to take a little somethin',
Colour of pills no matter
So long as we sweet-talkin',
Flashin' dem come-on-eyes,
Splashin' the night with laughter
And love-punch fire.

But when the pills no good
And you cryin' 'n tearin' the flowers
From your hair,
He give you white powder

### Stephanotis

To mend a broken heart.
It shoot through your veins like sun-light.
Then the sky so blue and
The stephanotis so dream-sweet
That you don't care that
The flowers are for funerals
And he put you in a white dress
To sell your black body.

JANE BEESON

# Cornerstone

There is someone beside me breathing deeply
his hand lies on my knee
his face is crumpled brown from the outdoors
his body is like a tree's trunk
his legs bony as the bones raised from peat.

Mostly we live gapped like posts
upright and distant, supporting our own load –
we speak little and seldom love.
Where is the fire that seared once.
Where the quick leap of passion.
I shall tell you of its change to gentle isolation –
I do not want closeness dragging me from my direction
– a bog with grass of bright emerald, lies.

My path is a sheep track over high ground –
for too long have I been another's cornerstone.

ALISON SPRITZLER-ROSE

# Bukovina

My world is gone: the brothels, rooming houses, the hunt.
I drifted off in a sleeper and the scenery left.
But I remember my dreams. A Jewess who said,
*Sir, I know our love is a little thing –*
*but so are stars, from here.*

Bullets too are little things. My limp remembers them.
Our hatreds were holy; we knew why
and whom we fought – the melody and the words.
Now the gentlemen are gone – so too, the wars.

I've been too long in this over-stuffed arm chair;
I am moulded to its penitent's horse-hair.
My tea has steeped to bitterness

But I see everything, now that the light is as dim
as the moon's reflection in a horse's eye.
I am far-sighted with age.
I see the anger of the oysters
in the pearls on lovely necks. My eyes
water in the cold to make the heavens clearer.

WILLIAM PALMER

# The Good Ship Empire

Here is a ship sailing on a cigar band,
red and gold and

blue the ocean. The captain appears.
He is a particularly hand-
some gentleman
asking where we

are bound? What particular course we are on?
The crew murmurs. Could it be
– could it? – that the hofficers emselves doan
no the corse we is on?

Send out birds, says Leftenant Aubergine.
They will report if the land

is fit to be landed upon.
If the grass rhymes with arse. A man
(like the fist of a ham
his huge head)
mounts the bridge and announces

Sir, we ave run aground. . .
On the blue-green

rocks. The faces reflected
in the ship's shadow
see, to their chagrin,
how, through their blond-bladed ripples,

the keel of the ship
is eating the sea-green pebbles

like peas on a series
of endless, impossible knives.

TREVOR McMAHON

# Honey

'Out of the strong came forth sweetness'

He had always been afraid
of bees but was pleased
to make the hives; precision,
order, satisfied him.

He would take no money,
and could not understand
what attracted her to them.

They took the new hive
to the bottom of the garden:
he was frightened, picking
at the string around his wrists.

She had no protection:
she took the queen between her lips;
the swarm bearded her chin.

CIARÁN RUBY

# The Carrickatine Disaster, First Anniversary November 1996

A year
on the cliff
and one
by one
in bitter
light
of Donegal
we lined
the empty
coffins of our
husbands
up against the
wall
and stooped
homeward

Women dark as
standing
stones
in unploughed
fields.

CLARE MACDONALD SHAW

# The Faust Family

They'll spider up this tower. Floodlights! Check
the guy-ropes, tense angles of taut from slack
so none of the six *funambules* will breakneck

into the night, falling off Saint-Michel.
On the nursery ropes, easy stunts. To go uphill
you slice your feet on wire, keep in bal-

-ance with a long bamboo; that's
the young boy. Clever sisters do the splits
or tip a chair on edge and sit. Must take guts,

we say, packed in the square as if
assembled for the guillotine, but tough
on the kids. Clap and cheer them off

uneasily. Now the hero steps up
into the belfry. Vanishes. Bats flap
out in a swarm, wheel and dip

over our screams. Look, he's got
himself hung upside-down from a foot-
strap. Slides to earth like the Tarot man, lit

by megawatts of moon. The star's here.
Cord round neck, she zips down wire
so fast her head haloes the sparks. Dare

and devil take the lilyliver!
Roars and groans from us; never
such nerve off-screen. And it's not over. . .

elder son will now rev and ride
his motorbike up Steelthread Road
(girl on the handlebars) and speed

down in reverse with her swung below.
Can't be done. They do it. We ask how –
screens, mirrors, mass hypnosis? Who

could live this life if it were real?
Either it's the rope-trick, western-style,
or the Faust family's been let out to scale

the Church again, hot from hell. No net
and no soft landing for the acrobat
pitted against old laws of gravity. What

makes them do it? After a fanfare thrill,
the last swallow-dive. We sigh, thin out, trail
off into back-streets, going solo by the canal

where leather Angels mass and wheel, but
can't lift off the ground. Cut through; get
the nerves fit again. Fear's a bad habit.

LEN KRISAK

# Gliding

How tenuous, you learn. The ice is thin
Where you had thought to skate forever. Trust
That seemed so obvious to you has cracked,
And where the cold once held, you've fallen in
And freeze. The way that you had thought it must,
This solid lake supported every line
You scrawled, each figure that you cut. In fact,
It was your silver slate. And now you find
You never really knew how sharp the blades
Might be that others write with; they were knives.
And like some naïf out of Currier and Ives,
You sink beneath the surface that we made
Of life. You've fallen through; no fate is worse.
Too bad that time won't travel in reverse.

ANGELA DOVE

# The Corset

I watch that fat old frog Diego spit
tobacco and arterial blood peppering his soft brown shoes.
The cockpit's dusty sacrum
is fenced by campesinos hookeyed with rough wine.
They lean inwards
as two inflated bags of feathers crow and scratch the clay.

I'm resting under the eaves of Frida Khalo's chocolate skirts.
Today she's dressed as a young girl
with white plumage and red carnations tasselling her hair.
I clasp her in my steel and linen cage
imprinted with bird's foot stitches
like the suture scars that stencil her wounded spine.

We return at night to the fine blue house in San Angel
where she gives birth to herself
through a tiny wound pouting on her thigh.
Then she paints her parturition.
Opening her body like a cupboard filled with icons.

JUDITH LAL

# Washing and Astronomy

There is a comet in the sky tonight. It trails in a sacred place,
somewhere between my knickers and your vest.

The last time it orbited the earth, Pharaohs were reproducing under fire-
signs. I bite my tongue. Patiently wait another two thousand years.

I am naked and my eye is stripped of glass,
as I peg, unpeg, with fingers that stick and unstick

these trousers with a life of their own,
blouses that conduct silent orchestras of grass.

The sky is alive with thousands of sleepless things,
and the moon, a nucleus, it hurts to look it straight in the eye,

a pristine, luminous melon, afloat in a black olive lake.
Too beautiful. Too complete in its roundness.

I know something has broken, it cracks
like a voice in confession and dents the concrete.

The night is clean. Sometimes my mother, it
croons and cradles. Sometimes my child, it comes undone.

ALEX SMITH

# The Madness of my Sister

The greengages turn to ice
in the conservatory; soon
they will be pure light.

Sun-rays yellow the panes.
Two o'clock.
Afternoons fall away like pearls
sliding off a broken string.

The endlessness of detail –
always to waste time. . .
I haven't washed my hair in weeks.

Another dress to put on,
another demand.
Whose body do I inhabit?

How quietly I am vanishing!

TOM BRYAN

# Dreaming, Babel

Isaak Emmanuilovich Babel had been dead twenty-seven years when I first met him in Moscow in 1968. I was 18. I am now 47 (the same age Babel was when last seen alive).

---

**Moscow, *Idaho*, Western USA that is.**

I was a student, supposedly studying petrochemical rock formations and the geology of undersea oil deposits. I lived in a wind-riven wooden house with several other students. The big house faced a tree-covered park, several blocks square. There were benches under the trees. I went to the benches to escape piles of unwashed dishes, loud stereos and arguments about revolution (for we all agreed that revolution or *counter-revolution* was coming).

The park had no real reason for being there since all the houses nearby already had big gardens and front lawns, full of wisteria or shrubs native to Scandinavia and Northern Europe, where most of the town founders came from a century or more before. One part of the park never changed. Near its western rim, was a row of tall fir trees. Through all the seasons, the evergreens changed colours only subtly, from lime to deep blue. There were hardwood trees too and in autumn, the bright dead leaves swirled and rustled around the park, under the benches and around your feet. Squirrels would gather pine cones, sniff the benches, then scurry away. From any corner of the park, you saw the snow-covered mountains. Local children played in the park, riding bikes, sledding, throwing snowballs. Many of them were blonder than snow, dressed in thick parkas and fur boots. I only remember the children in snow because I was never in the park in the summer, the only season sure to be free of snow. It bothers me too that I never learned the names of the hardwood trees. I vividly remember the Douglas Fir trees – maybe just because I knew their names. The other trees just fade away when I try to recall them.

---

I met Babel in Moscow, this way. I went to a lecture by locally-born Katinka Ivanovich, a teacher of Russian.

"Babel (she said it BAH byeel) was an outsider, a Jewish intellectual from Odessa who rode out with the Red Cavalry, on Gorki's advice, to gather experience of real life in order to improve his short story writing, Isaak Babel described that brutal life with clarity and fairness, but always as an outsider. His stories had great appeal at the time, but they later got him into trouble with Stalin."

"What happened to Babel?"

"Nobody knows. He vanished in one of Stalin's purges. Many think Stalin killed as many Jews as Hitler did. All the books mention him 1894?–1939? or *circa,* 1941. Russia was being attacked by Hitler, and hundreds of thousands of Russians were starving. Maybe Babel just disappeared with the rest, into a mass grave. His works were proscribed, but revived after Stalin's death." She described how Babel took the reader into the sights, aromas and intrigues of the Odessa ghetto; its Rabbis, gangsters, dock workers.

I went to the library but his name was missing from every collection of Russian short stories.

I went to Katinka Ivanovich's office but she laughed when I told her. "Babel has *truly* vanished, the world over. He was only recently translated into English. Here. Take this 'Odesskiye Rasskazy' with English translation. Keep it as long as you wish."

"Thank you," I said in Russian. She grinned.

---

**Odessa is a dark dancer, in bright blue skirt, white blouse. She dances to the old Jewish music of the ghetto. Under her skirt are great red petticoats, rustling and sometimes sticking to her dark sweating thighs. She is barefoot and**

**leaps onto the tables, inviting all to shelter under her red petticoats. Many go under, eagerly, except one dark shy boy with glasses. He is in the corner writing nervously. He would like to go under the petticoat, he is throbbing for it but he fears the heady perfume there, he fears he would pass out under its fragrance, then never wake up . . .**

So, he stays in the corner, writing, watching, blushing. Stepping near the dancer but always out of reach of her dizzying skirts.

---

Me. **Why Babel?** Babel was the outsider who did not feel superior to the cruel laughing cavalrymen who killed, loved and laughed. He felt inferior to them. I know the feeling.

I, Michael Klein

My father was Jewish, but not an intellectual, a doctor or professor. He was a stevedore on the docks in Portland, Oregon. He was never a practising Jew and I myself knew nothing about religion. My old man, David, was a kind of working-class intellectual. He had a huge wall chart up in our bathroom. It had all the bones of the human body highlighted. He broke so many bones while working on the waterfront that he labelled each one on the chart: **"Metacarpal, broken June 1967 unloading bananas from Ecuador."** I thought he was trying to break every bone in his body before he died. Then I suppose, he would just vanish into the wall chart.

I am thin, short, and dark and wear glasses: a city boy in an agricultural town where everyone seems tall and blonde. In truth, the people here are friendly and I have no reason to feel so cut off from them.

**Why Babel?**

Remember, this is 1968, Paris, Chicago, Prague. The whole world is erupting and there is nowhere safe. You can feel it in the air. The Cossacks *are* coming. The Czars of the world are frightened. They are sending out the troops. I had trouble concentrating on petrochemicals when I could almost hear the clatter of horse hooves coming through the park.

Portland was just like Odessa. Awash with Russians and Africans, Burnside Avenue full of all the hoboes just off the western boxcars, wintering over in this city, a wet but warmer place. Street preachers, great black men in turbans, cowboys, Indians, Chinese, Vietnamese, sailors, drifters. Something always faintly sinister and apocalyptic about it. For me, it was an easy dream-shift to Odessa:

**Babel and I are soaking it up. The rich aroma of wheat, sugar and wool from the teeming docks. In the ghetto, young violinists are practising the same notes over and over again. Zimbalist. Heifitz. "Jascha, Mein Liebling, keep up the work and you will go all over the world with that violin." Babel and I, almost physical twins, duck down alleys, steal from fruit stalls when we are hungry, absorbing the stories from fishwives, pimps, sailors, gangsters, but always, one ear cocked to the wind. Maybe you would hear hooves on the cobbles first, or see dust in the distance, or hear guns and whips and harsh guttural cries in other languages. Pogroms and Jew baiting to keep the unruly elements happy and diverted. Babel and I slip into the corners, with scorpions, until the troops pass. When it is safe, the dancing woman comes out, her red petticoats swirling in the sultry air of Odessa.**

---

Odessa seeped into my Moscow, between the ploughing and harvesting and oceans of wheat from the great Palouse country. Midnight walks down long streets between pickup trucks, past Country and Western bars and Chinese restaurants, in wind so cold my snot would freeze, and stay frozen, until I could thaw it hours later with the steam from a coffee mug. Many of the students had been loggers and lumberjacks and took me in tow, out of pity. Johnny Loggins put it bluntly:

"It's time you lost your cherry you little runt. I know just the place."

Loggins *knew* the place. A logging town about thirty miles away. Friday night. Six of us crammed into Loggins' rusted Chevy Impala. The house was a huge three-storey wooden house in the centre of town. It had a swing on the wrap-around wooden porch. Loggins bounded up the stairs, banged on the doors, and lights came on. We went into the hall. Peacock feathers, stuffed beavers. A huge grizzly bear head grinned down at me. Loggins shoved me into a room, then they all disappeared too.

A woman removed my glasses and all I saw then was a huge dark shape looming over me. Cut. *Thanks* Loggins, for nuthin. Bang on the door. The rest of the bunch, smirking, grinning.

Loggins stuck out a huge hand. "Welcome to manhood, Klein. Yer one of *us* now."

One of them. I never told Loggins *nothing* happened in that room smelling of nicotine, stale beer and makeup. The huge woman merely fell asleep but kept me awake all night with her snoring. Dawn couldn't come fast enough. I walked down the long wooden steps with my own variety of Cossacks. I wish Babel could have been there.

---

The copy of Babel was well-worn and the binding had broken. As a result, the pages were falling out. I took it to Katinka Ivanovich and offered to pay for it but she just laughed and told me to keep it as I had *earned* it.

---

I was sitting in the park in late spring. Fallen leaves from the hardwoods blew across the park, now noisy with children's laughter and birdsong. Sun reached the ground, coming through in biblical shafts. I was hardly aware of someone sitting on the far end of my bench.

"Babel? I like him too."

I looked up. Christine Olaffson. I knew her but we had never spoken. I stuttered. "He . . . hello. Are you studying Russian?"

"No. My mother is good friends with Katinka Ivanovich and Babel is *her* religion. She passes out his books like Gideon Bibles, but I'm a willing convert."

"You live near here, don't you?"

"I've lived here all my life. My father sells farm machinery. Tell me, they say Babel just vanished, disappeared."

"Nobody really knows," I said.

"It is the outsider in Babel I identify with. Babel never belonged *anywhere.* In the ghetto. In the army. The Revolution. The Soviet. Maybe he just walked away from it all." When Christine said "walked away from it all" she rubbed her foot through the dead leaves.

"I don't think so. Katinka Ivanovich says there are now papers which proved Babel died in a concentration camp. Anyway, you're not an outsider. You're part of the town."

She laughed. "You mean, I'm tall, blonde and Swedish Lutheran? You can live in a place all your life and never feel part of it. My mother was born in Sweden but left her village when she was ten. We visited a few years ago. My mother couldn't remember much and felt a total outsider. I fit right in and was speaking Swedish in a week. I felt as though *I* had gone home, not my mother."

She go up to go.

I'll see you again. The Isaak Babel Restoration Society."

She laughed and waved, disappearing down the long dark tunnel of fir trees. I went to the park the next few days but Christine wasn't there. Then, it was time for me to go back to Portland for the summer.

---

I remembered a strange thing though. The first time I had ever really noticed Christine Olaffson was one spring day in the park, a few years before. She had on one of these billowing floral peasant dresses. The wind blew and I could see her petticoats swirling. They were red.

---

I returned to the park and town on a golden September day. I plucked up courage to knock on Christine's front door.

Her mother came to the door.

"Christine worked all summer. The last we've heard, she worked in New York City, on her way to Sweden."

"Thanks," I mumbled.

Trouble was, my old man decided to add to his broken bone collection by dropping a stevedore's hook on his head, breaking his skull in three places. I needed to help out at home so had to drop out of my petrochemical studies, which, I must admit, had suffered greatly after I met Babel.

---

I never got to return to that park. I am now the same age as Babel when he went missing. Ah, Babel, the clouds rolled over Odessa, over the dock, over the wool and sugar, the Yiddish and Russian, over and under the petticoats of the brown dancers. The Cossacks never came that final time. We never heard their horses.

---

I could never vanish. Friends and family would miss me. The state has names and numbers for me in their computers. I have my own books, photos, videos. A man could not vanish today. Could he? Surely not, it is impossible.

Yet, that park has vanished. The wheat fields and fine Indian ponies are gone. Christine Olaffson is gone. And they will vanish completely when my memories of them are gone. And Babel, when this story is written, you too will have vanished into that grey gulag again. Da Svidanya. Farewell.

We leave home.

We seek home.

Then, we vanish.

ALAN TUPPEN

# Summer Lightning

Where the Sungei Sating flows down out of the jungle and into the South China Sea stands the small town of Batu Itam. A couple of miles up the coast is a beach where every year the giant turtles haul their bulk out of the water to lay their eggs. At one time every beach for a hundred miles in each direction was so favoured, but thanks to dogs and the Malay fondness for turtle eggs, this is the only one left. Today the stretch of sand has been developed into a tourist attraction so that one can no longer just wander onto the beach at night and witness this primeval marvel. But twenty years ago everything was more casual, and only a huddle of reed huts stood where the concrete and glass hotel is now. A hut could be rented for a few dollars a night and one could eat rice and fried fish that had been caught from the boat pulled up on the sand in front of the huts. It was hardly cordon bleu or even varied, but it was fresh. In those days Batu Itam was smaller and sleepier than it is today. There were just two hotels, neither with the sort of facilities that hotels today think it necessary to offer. They offered a clean bed and security, which to many travellers were the only things that mattered.

Conroy chose the New Pelican, not through recommendation or inspection, but just because he preferred the name, wondering what the Old Pelican had been like. The hotel had been built in colonial days, and the once white facade was streaked and stained with green and brown. He pushed open the street door and climbed the stairs to a door with a frosted glass window marked "Reception". He knocked and at first there was no reply. From inside came the sound of someone searching the airwaves with an old, old wireless set, but after a few seconds the whining and crackling stopped, and he could hear the flapping of sandals as their owner shuffled to the door. It opened to reveal a Chinese of indeterminate age, wearing baggy shorts and a stained vest. Expressionless, he survey Conroy for a second, then asked.

"You want room?"

"Yes."

"One night, ten dollar. You stay how many night?"

"I don't know. Two, three."

The man grunted and shuffled off.

"Come."

Conroy followed him through another door to find himself looking over a decayed garden. The hotel was built round a small courtyard with a pool at its centre, and the two men were passing along a sort of galleried landing overlooking it. As he went, the other flapped an arm at doors.

"Shower. Toilet."

Abruptly he stopped and pushed open a door. The room was dark, having only a shuttered window facing the courtyard and a ventilator high up on the opposite wall. Inside were only a bed, table and chair, and Conroy was relieved to see that there was a mosquito net. He could imagine the vengeful hordes rising from the pool after sundown, and brown splashes on the net and wall round the bed confirmed his suspicion. The other turned to him.

"Room OK?"

"OK."

"You pay now one night."

Conroy dug into his pocket and fished out a ten dollar note. The man took it and without a word slapped back to his radio. Conroy put his bag on the table and switched on the ceiling fan. It groaned and swung alarmingly from side to side so that he felt he had better switch if off again. He couldn't tell whether the sheets on the bed were clean, and didn't really care. In this climate he would be sweating again within minutes of showering. It was no wonder no one ever hurried in this country, the human body couldn't handle it. Just climbing the stairs had made him stream, so he flopped on the chair, not feeling too well. What with the spicy food and the heat he felt weak, his stomach queasy, and his skin felt greasy and gritty. He sighed, and without getting up, leaned over, unzipped his bag and pulled out a towel, clean shirt and underpants. He would have to make an effort to stand up and walk to the shower on the off-chance that it worked. As he got up, a cockroach scuttled out from under the bed and he aimed a foot at it. He was surprised to hit it and felt a little better. It was strange how cockroaches seemed to shrink when one killed them; already it seemed smaller. He kicked the body into a corner and locked the door behind him. The shower room was dim and the walls were slimy, but the cool water refreshed him and he realised he was hungry.

Emerging onto the landing, Conroy could see that the sun was low. No part of the courtyard was lit, only the top of the wall on the east side still catching the sun. Faintly he could hear cries from outside in the street as stalls were being set up and children were coming noisily home from school.

In his room, ants had found the dead cockroach, and a small army of them was swarming round it, tugging it one way and another. They were the smallest ants he had ever seen, and were running up and down the wall to a crack behind the table. He sat down and watched them for a minute. They had tipped the insect onto its side and were trying to drag it bodily up the wall, presumably in an attempt to pull it through the crack to their nest. It slid back down, and at once the ants busied themselves tipping it back up again. Again it collapsed and again the ants set about trying to drag it up the wall. Conroy stood up, threw his thin linen jacket over one shoulder and stepped outside. The sun had set as fast as it can only in the tropics. The humid air in the courtyard was still, and the barely audible whine of mosquitos came up to him from its dank, leafy depths. Quickly he descended the stairs to the street.

The shops were still open, but now lit by bare light bulbs and paraffin lamps. Small boys fanned flies off fruit, meat and sticky sweet cakes. Families were out walking or sitting round tables pulled out onto the pavement, the air full of noise and the smell of spicy cooking. At the end of the street and across the road that ran alongside the river, the ground sloped down to the water and was planted with trees strung with light bulbs. More stalls were laid out there, all lit with flaring paraffin lamps and accompanied by blaring transistor radios. As Conroy crossed over, he could see canoes tied up at the river bank, loaded with goods whose identity he could only guess at, hidden in the shadows as they were. He seemed to be the only foreigner there, but the crowds around him shot him only the occasional inquisitive glance. It was cooler down here by the river, and his hunger had intensified, so when he found a food stall with an empty table he sat down. There was no menu, and he was looking over to see what people on neighbouring tables were eating when the stall holder came over holding a ladle in one hand and a palm frond fan in the other.

"Want eat, Mister?"

"Yes please."

"What you want? Satay? Chicken? Mee, noodle?"

"Yes."

"OK. I make, one minute."

And little more than a minute later the man put on his table a plate of noodles spiced with chillies, with four slivers of bamboo laid on top, each threaded with chunks of grilled chicken, followed by a small dish of an ochre paste.

"Sauce for satay," announced the man, "You like?"

The sharp sweet scent of the chillies mingled with the aroma of the chicken.

"Yes, I like it very much, thank you."

The man smiled, nodded and turned back to his cooking.

Conroy picked a pair of chopsticks from the glass on the table and was about to start eating when he became aware of a man watching him from a neighbouring table. He looked up and the man smiled.

"American?" he asked.

"No," Conroy replied. "English."

The other man's smile widened a little.

"You go many places? Many countries?"

"A few."

"You like here?"

"Yes, very peaceful, beautiful. This is my first time here, I came to Batu Itam to see the turtles."

"Yes, all farang come Batu Itam see turtles."

The man took a sip of his tea.

"How you think my country?"

Conroy didn't answer straight away, but took a good look at him. Could be Malay or Chinese, he thought, face half in shadow, light from the lamps in the trees reflected in one eye. Mid-forties, thick jet black hair, thin moustache. Conroy considered how he should answer. He remembered how in South Korea when he had been visiting a temple in a famous beauty spot, a group of students had asked him the same question, but only when they had steered him away from any people or buildings and into the trees, and even then they had kept a watch for anyone coming. Things here didn't seem oppressive at all, but he knew the authorities frowned on open criticism, and that in some countries the government planted agents provocateurs to trap those unwise enough to open their mouths too wide, just as they used undercover agents to trap drug users and dealers. As he was considering, a young woman came over and sat with the man, putting a bowl in front of him and another for herself. He said a few words to her, and Conroy caught the word "Inggeris" and smiled at the couple. The man indicated vaguely.

"My wife, she understands a few words inggeris."

She smiled shyly and started to eat. Conroy took a mouthful too, the food now not too hot, and for a minute they all ate, then the man spoke again.

"How long you stay my country?"

"Oh, three weeks, then I go back to England."

"You see Singapore, Penang, Melaka?"

"Not yet, this is my first week."

The man nodded but said nothing, and they all set to eat again. The woman finished first and said a few words to her husband. He looked up and held out his hand to Conroy.

"I am Hassan. When you finish, we go back my house, drink beer, OK?"

Conroy was surprised. He had often been engaged in conversation over a meal or a drink, and often invited to a bar or a place of less repute, but seldom to anyone's house, and for the woman to apparently make the suggestion was amazing.

When they had finished eating, the three of them walked into the night, the woman walking quietly behind them, as Hassan guided Conroy through the dark streets, away from the shops and brightly lit places into quiet lanes where the glow of lanterns could be seen shining softly from behind matting screens in the houses. Here, where the people lived, the houses were on stilts, built lightly of wood and lath, with matting at doors and windows to allow cooling air to pass without hindrance. Family groups sat on verandas and steps, and from time to time a greeting would be called softly through the night air.

"Salaam."

And Hassan would return the call, bowing slightly. At length they arrived and climbed the steps to Hassan's house.

"We are honoured by the farang guest in our house," he told Conroy, gesturing him to sit on a cushion by the wall. He turned to his wife, raising his fingers to his mouth in a mime of eating, and she immediately disappeared behind a matting partition, to reappear very soon with a tray of drinks with two glasses and some fruit. For a while they drank in silence, then Conroy, feeling increasingly awkward, leaning towards Hassan and told him, "In fact it is I who am honoured by your hospitality."

He looked around at the bright cushions, low bamboo furniture, and up into the dimly lit rafters.

"I like your house."

Hassan smiled and translated for his wife.

Conroy went on, "Western houses have too many things in them, we are . . ." he seemed to be searching for the right word, "hindered by things. But of course conditions are different, people have different expectations."

"I think so," Hassan said, "I have see them in magazines and movies. To me they not look comfortable. Our life here, it is different. We, our people, we do not ask much, but our children, they are not like us. They see your ways, your goods, they must have them too. It is great sadness."

He took a draught.

"I have two sons. They grow up, now they go Kuala Lumpur look for work. Not happy stay here, say we old fashioned. Maybe."

He stared into his glass, and Conroy began to feel uncomfortable again, wondering where this was leading, but Hassan was speaking again.

"I think you good man. You have children?"

"Unfortunately no, and last year my wife . . . we were divorced."

"I am sorry, maybe you should have child, then no divorce."

Conroy sighed, "Yes, maybe, but now it's too late."

"Not too late. You find other woman. Every man should have son, for his old age. You have good job?"

"I'm an engineer."

Yes, good job. My job not so good, manager palm oil plantation, but lucky, here many men no job, do a little fishing, odd job here and there. You know. Many farang, they come here, see many men with no job, think they lazy. Not so. When I young man, I have three job. In day I drive rickshaw and at night I cook food or I go fishing, and my wife, she do cleaning and washing. Then I get job at plantation, Allah be praised."

He smiled and opened another beer.

"You no see turtle yet, right?"

Conroy was surprised at this shift in the conversation.

"No, not yet, I was planning to take a bus out to the beach tomorrow."

But Hassan put a hand on Conroy's arm.

"Never mind, we go now, I know best place, I take you."

Outside, the air was cooler, velvety smooth, the faint smell of fires and vegetation, the sound of the distant surf all but drowned by the incessant cicadas and the burble of frogs. Mosquitos whined in and out of his hearing, but unable to see then, Conroy resigned himself to being bitten. Low over the jungle a huge moon hung, illuminating their faces and casting long shadows that seemed to become inextricably tangled. Hassan dived behind the house and reappeared at the wheel of a small jeep.

"Company car," he announced with a wry smile, "Please get in."

Conroy went to climb in the back, but Hassan's wife waved him into the front with a smile and got into the back herself.

Little by little the sound of the sea grew, until suddenly they emerged out of the trees and onto the beach, the sea silver and black beyond the sand. In the moonlight the scene had an ethereal beauty, like a film set. Where the waves stirred the sand in their breaking, motes of light danced in the tumbling water, and Conroy stared in wonder.

"Maybe we are lucky tonight," Hassan broke in, and fished out a torch from under the dash of the jeep. He didn't switch it on, but scanned up and down the beach, listening intently. Here the surf was king, the cicadas that had all but drowned out the other sounds back among the trees, only a background themselves now. At their feet the sand above the high water mark was pocked with black shadows like the surface of the moon, but below the line the moonlight reflected in a sheen on the wet sand. Hassan started off up the beach, torch still unlit in his hand, and shortly Conroy could just pick out a dark mass on the sand and hear a faint wheezing. As they drew near, he could see that the mass was in fact a large turtle, already half way up the beach, its tracks plain where the waves had not wiped them away. Hassan stopped a couple of yards away.

"Now we wait," he whispered, "not disturb."

Conroy could hardly believe the effort the creature was expending for such little result. He had seen film of turtles in the sea, and there they were swift and ruthless hunters, to be avoided. But here, on land, each concerted movement of its limbs moved it only a few inches, and then it had to pause and gather its strength for the next few. And so it toiled up the sand, apparently oblivious to the three watchers, until it seemed to Conroy that it would never get where it was going. But then, ponderously, it turned around, and with its back feet started to fling sand away from it until it had dug a hole maybe a foot deep. When it paused, Hassan moved forward and positioned himself so that he could reach down, and suddenly the eggs started dropping into the hole, only for the man to scoop them out as they fell and lay them in a pile beside him on the sand. They were large, white and translucent like huge pearls, and when Hassan handed one up, Conroy was surprised to find it warm and leathery. Hassan's wife was putting them into a bag, and when they had a dozen or so, Hassan got up and rejoined Conroy.

"We leave her some babies, not take all," he smiled.

Conroy was hesitant. "I thought you were not allowed to take the eggs."

"Oh, this beach public, not protected, but not many turtle. Our custom, you know. My father, my father father, his father, all take egg, I have right."

Conroy realised the turtle had finished laying its eggs and was laboriously refilling the hole, pushing sand back in to bury the remaining eggs. At last, with a sigh, the creature started to drag its bulk back down to the water, infinitely slowly, exhausted now its task was completed. Conroy noticed its eyes were wet, apparently with tears from the huge exertion of it all, and he felt suddenly sad that he had witnessed what should surely have been a private affair, but equally he could see it could never be hidden. If a tank had driven up out of the sea and over the beach it could not have been more obvious, so distinctively the sand bore its tracks. Even if they had missed the actual event, it would have been easy to find and dig up the eggs. Hassan picked up a dead palm frond and started sweeping sand to smooth out the tracks.

"Maybe some baby live," he muttered. "You see how hard she work, like me, many hour little money."

And unexpectedly his wife spoke too.

"People like turtle, we work hard for little, we cry but no one see or listen. But you know Mr Conroy, all life like that. If we have easy time we do nothing. We struggle for everything. We must. You will see. For each other, to keep what we have. To be alive is to struggle. Turtle understand."

The turtle had reached the water's edge and sat just letting the waves break over it for a minute, then refreshed, it heaved itself forward and vanished into the dark water. Hassan and his wife turned and headed for the jeep. Humbled, Conroy realised he still held the egg Hassan had handed him. He sank to his knees and dug down into the warm sand as deep as he could and gently laid the egg there, refilling the hole and smoothing over the top. As he rose to his feet, he glanced up through the trees behind the beach. The blue flickers on the horizon betrayed the summer lightning among the far distant peaks. Turning, he could just discern a faint line of brightness way across the water in advance of the new day. Feeling strangely cleansed, he hurried down the beach after his friends.

SUHAYL SAADI

# Rabia

I fell in love with Rabia the first time I saw her in the Old Bazaar. It was a fleeting glimpse, through the crystalline air of mid-winter, a flourish between stalls and amongst the massed flesh of anonymous faces, hands, lips. Yet enough for a lifetime. And beyond.

I was seventeen at the time and had been sent by my mother to buy provisions for the household. Some distant relatives from the town of Leh were coming to visit, and we needed almost three times the usual amount of food, not to mention gifts with which to make them feel welcome as guests. It was a strange time of year to be travelling. Snow and ice competed with each other to see which might cover more of the world, while the sun gave off heat like an impoverished aristocrat. We hadn't seen these relatives for years – they had never known me, and my mother and father had last met them when they were all children. They would be bringing their entire family along, and so in a few days' time, I would be greeting long-lost cousins as well as aunts and uncles of whom I had heard only through tales. Over the years, they had become fictions in my head, and then myths, so that a little apprehension was mixed in with the curiosity I felt at their impending arrival. It was in this rather pensive mid-winter mood that I set off early that morning for the old Jumma Bazaar.

The sun had not yet risen and a pale milk light flitted uneasily between the shadows. The houses were all shuttered-up and only the occasional clatter of servants' shoes on stone issuing from within the haveli broke the gray dream slumber of the morning. The air was cold glass in my throat. I pulled my shawl more tightly around my shoulders and walked quickly to keep warm. There were two bazaars in our town. The Old Bazaar had been there since before living memory. Some said that Dungpa Miru had strolled among its noisy stalls, and haggled with its Afghani traders. The Afghans, like the Yehudi, went everywhere, lending money and selling jewellery, and always making a profit for though charging interest is against Islam, they seemed somehow to be able to circumvent this legality. They travelled from the great twin rivers of the West, all the way across the land of Fars, and had been known in Rangoon and Tibet. Most of the merchants, however, were white-robed Hindus from the lands of Kush, far to the south. (But I digress, as has become my habit, over the years.) As I drew closer to the Bazaar, there was still no sign of any activity. I might have been the only person in the town. However, the moment the narrow mud streets expanded into the open square, it was as though I had emerged into a world at the very instant of its creation. A jangling hub-hub, the mountain devils danced the dance of the soul upon the old stone slabs, and the joyous bustle of humanity around me was like the breath of the saints upon my skin. Everyone was wrapped in furs and woollens: ankle-length chughas of thick, black material shorn from the long-haired sheep of Baltistan; bristling flying-fox headgear with flaps pulled down over the ears; boots of pale brown fur. The people of my town knew how to dress against the cold. They had learned to survive the high winters of the mountain valleys. Even though that morning there was no wind, yet the silent ice of the day stole between people, through the fissures in their skin, the picot of their soul.

I had a list of provisions to buy, and a large sack in which to carry them, and I set about my task with the vigour of winter. It was as I was bargaining with a Tajik merchant for some beshak shirin melons (it was customary to offer guests something sweet on their arrival, and these delicious melons would be ideal) that I first caught sight of Rabia. Of course, I didn't know her name then (although later, I felt I had always known it). She passed by, a figure on the edge of my vision, on the precipice of the morning. A fleeting figure in black. Green eyes. A russet lock, brushing her cheek. The warmth within the snow skin of honey and milk, winter's beauty, and the promise of rubies, living and breathing as lips. The perfect, dizzying curve of a bird's flight from mountain-top. My breath stopped and became one with the frozen air. Things seemed not to exist. Only time, hanging by a thread from the sky, stood between the entity that was me, and Rabia. The blade of creation fell. I looked up. She was gone. The merchant had been speaking to me. I had missed most of what he had said. I managed to catch up with the conversation, but my mind was elsewhere. Today I would not be able to strike a good bargain, I knew. I didn't care. It had ceased to matter. The morning had become filled with the face of a woman I had never met. Was not even sure existed. And yet, already I knew her name. I had named her, just as when I was a child, I had named all things. For me, she was Rabia, the girl of the mountains, the fleeting gazelle of the plains (though at that time I had set eyes on neither plains nor gazelle, yet I had heard much of both from the long tongues of old women and travelling merchants). For the rest of the morning, I was utterly distracted even more so than the yellow-robed lamas who came to beg in the bazaar, every Jumma. I purchased provisions haphazardly, so that it took twice as long as usual, and my body felt unsure of itself, suddenly clumsy in the subtle mountain air. Every so often, my heart would bounce against my ribs as though it were trying to escape from the confines of my body. It too, longed to soar with the bird, to peck at the sky, to swell in emptiness. But in the emptiness I was not alone, for Rabia had grown to fill everything for me. She was the first glint of sun across the spines of cliffs, the warm swish of her black, tribal costume, perpetuated in a thousand identical market-place mornings, the sweet taste of her lips in every grain of golden halvah. O my Rabia! Where was she? Even though she was all, yet I longed to touch her, to reach her presence, as I must have longed for life in the time before I was born.

When the relatives arrived, I was scarcely interested. What should have been the event of the year became for me just another manifestation of a love which I knew was the blood in my heart but which, like that blood, I was unable to grasp, to let flow between the tips of my fingers. Their Ladakhi accents reminded me of the gentle tinkle of Rabia's voice. Animated conversations would pass above and below me across the sandali and I would nod and smile, but I was thinking only of the caravan which I knew at that moment would be travelling by the low bank of a frozen river. My thoughts, the icicles of the glass waterfall at its source. As it melted a little during the day, yet it would freeze again at night, so that throughout the winter, it never changed. And in a thousand drops of ice, was my Rabia reflected. I even attempted to find out more about her from my relatives. Obliquely, I questioned them about the caravan which I was certain had set off from their land. But they had heard nothing of such a caravan. I did not dare ask about Rabia. Partly from fear of arousing their – and my parents' – suspicions, and partly because I felt she was my secret and I did not wish to share her with anyone. Even if that meant that I would never see her again. Strange, how love can destroy those it attracts, that it may live. In stinging, the bee commits suicide.

Winter lightened into spring, the almond and rose trees began to blossom, and strawberries became ripe for the picking. The men went up into the high crags where they blew sonorous notes from the mouths of long, wooden horns. Even these loping, invisible notes, for me followed the gracious gait of my beloved across the empty stillness. I thought they might summon her back from the frozen waterfalls of the land of the Dards, back to where the ice had broken up into tiny, white floes which seethed with the current far below.

*In the meadow, in the meadow, in the higher meadow blows –*
*listen, lad, O listen to my song –*
*A flower, far the sweetest that in field and garden grows –*
*listen, lad, listen to my song.*

*Thou mayest cull the flower, sweetheart, thou mayest cull the tender flower,*
*But thou shalt not grasp it rudely in thine hand;*
*Else 'twill wither in a moment, 'twill be perished in an hour,*
*If thou, ruthless, dare to seize it in thine hand.*
*O, but, lean thy bosom t'wards it, it will nestle to thy soul,*
*It will cling with tend'rest tendrils round thine heart:*
*Ah, lad, lean thy bosom t'wards it, it will grow into thy soul,*
*And with strong, yet tender tendrils, hold thine heart.*

As the sun's power strengthened and life began to burst out everywhere, I grew weaker. I ate less and less, finding that only a little halvah and goat's milk and the tenderest pieces of lamb would suffice my diminishing appetite. My mother became worried, and took me to see a Yunani physician. I was given a liquid distilled from some foul-tasting herbs which I pretended to swallow but actually spat out as soon as their heads were turned. I had no wish to recover from the love which had possessed me. My obsession had become my life.

I waited for summer's warmth to clear the mountain passes, for I had resolved to go in search of my beloved. Secretly one night, I stole away from my house, my town, the valley which was the only world I had known, and climbed the high path, heading eastwards. I had as my guides, the moon which waxed and waned through the night and across the months, and the stars which pullulated from behind their burqa. The night was my Rabia's cloak, the day, her shining eyes, the sunrise and sunset, the matched clasp of her lips. Every swaying branch of every tree I passed, beckoned me on, higher and higher, each nod of a flower confirmed my course as surely as any map. I could not read at that time, so what use would a map have been? The land, the streams, the sky were my maps; I read them like a manuscript, rolled out before me in sound, colour, smell, touch and taste. Like a farmer, I tasted the soil and knew where I was going; like a minstrel, the notes of the wind spoke to me in a wordless tongue; the quality of the dew upon my lips changed every morning and by this, I trod as a hunter might, with deft steps, risking all in the certainty of the chase. When I prayed, it was on the summits of mountains. My heart seemed closer to Rabia at these moments; the air, diamond clear with my longing.

I was in one of those high mountain villages during the festival of Eid al Azha. A lamb was readied to be sacrificed, and I was given the honour of performing the Qurbani. I took hold of the curved blade, newly-cut on the grindstone. It was winter again, and the sharp light of the sun sliced through the pale blue mantle of the sky as it must surely do, in heaven. I could feel the heart's blood of the lamb pulse faster beneath my fingers as I took hold of its neck. With one, swift stroke, I opened the great vein. Blood the colour of love gushed over my hands, turning snowflakes into rubies. It is said that when a lamb is sacrificed in memory of Hazrat Ibrahim's great act, the last thing the animal sees is a vision of Paradise. The fading light in the lamb's eyes as it bled into oblivion, that was the longing of my heart for Rabia.

After many months of travel, living off the land and as the guest of the people of countless isolated villages, I came at last to the land of Ladakh. All around me, I felt the wailing of Dards and Mons and the battle-cries of the Yellow Lamas as they drew the blood of the Red Lamas. In these high lands, the Great Khans of Tibet vied with fat Buddha stones and the invisible, omniscient God of my own folk. For a while my own land of Baltistan was entirely Musselman, the peoples to the east adhered to many different faiths. Strange rock-carvings and cryptic flower-symbols became part of my map, and I tasted the wine of paganism on my journey. I was certain that my love had passed through all these lands, had partaken of the same cartograph in which I now immersed myself. Rabia, I knew, was born of the fire of faith, she was hewn from the rock and stone of this high world, she poured herself from the goatskin gourd with every intoxicating drop of liquor. It was she, in the cry of the muezzin across the endless chasm of time. And when I had passed through all of these, had tasted of everything and more, then would I re-unite with those enticing green eyes, that silken voice, the gentle tread of delicate feet. Then would I leap off the cliff and not fall, not be smashed on the rocks below. Then would I soar for miles, for years, in Rabia and with her at the same time. We would fly together over the world's roof.

I became a great traveller, a chronicler of humanity and of nature (during the course of which, I finally learned to read and write). I was known as *Son of Ibn Battuta*, which was a great honour, and yet none of my admirers, nor yet any of my family (who were now treated almost like royalty in their home town) knew of my real quest. Not a soul was aware of that gray morning back when I was barely out of childhood, and none had been permitted to glimpse my source, my beloved, my Rabia.

Perhaps some day, I will find her. My heart tells me that I must find her. I am not yet old, but one day, I shall (God Willing) acquire the wisdom of the idiots which age engenders. And then perhaps, I may glimpse her once again. I sometimes wonder whether if, at the moment of my death, I will see her face, if that image, the poem which contains everything and that which beyond everything, will be imprinted upon my soul as I leave this world and journey into the next. Into Rabia. All that I have done, each thought that I have thought, every one of my actions have been consequences merely, of that moment which lies outside time and which is therefore eternal. It has defined my life, and it will carve my death. I have never left the Old Bazaar, but am still there, waiting for her to return. Even as night falls.

GEORGE BURNS

# Blue Vanishing Monday

We are in a club in the city. The Friday Karma. It is always the Friday Karma. Friday, Saturday, Sunday, makes no difference. China Zones is blasting out over the speakers. We are totally tranced you know. Totally booma darooma mabaya. Me, Sparks and Dizzy. Strobe lights oscillating on jerky heads in the claustrophobic pleasuredrome. Green, blue, red, yellow and back to green, faces and bodies gyrating, shifting ground, wriggling. Anorexic puppets with glazed eyes on E, Eccies, in the Temazepam Holy Land.

Dizzy is small and cute, and has some Amyl Nitrite and Sasha King. The gorgeous Sasha with the silly shrill voice, all sweetness and completely out of order violence. And he knows she likes pain. They gravitate toward each other. Dizzy and the weird bitch. Jerk, jerk, jerk. Heads bobbing. Green, blue, red, yellow and back to green. Chemical bonding. Valency from bobbing heads. He knows, she knows, no preliminaries.

They, Dizzy and Sasha, have gone by four. They have gone to a secret back court behind the tenements on the west side of the city, known locally as the wedding bed.

At half past four Sparks has had enough and we are off up the long and winding road. But Sparks is different tonight. He keeps saying things in Italian.

– I love this fucking city.

He tells me, and it is tonight for Dizzy.

–Però il clima del settentrione.

– Fuck off. What?

I'm telling him and he falls into silence.

– No but, listen.

Sparks starts up again.

– I mean what do you do when you get to fifty and you can't see any fucking future for yourself?

I'm speechless, mainly because I'm not sure what he's on about.

– This? What is all this anyway? Life? Why should it be so fucking miserable? Whose idea was that?

I look about myself still unable to comprehend.

– Una camera con vista, sulla citta.

– I want better than this Cal. I don't just want to graduate, go to work, get paid, get laid and jerk off at the Friday Karma every weekend. I deserve better. Fuck, no, we deserve better.

I do know what he means. I mean he's right, in a way. I mean it is so senseless. Weekend after weekend. No progress. But when you get down to it and think about it long and hard – I mean really long and really hard – you would just go totally out of the box. Sometimes I just lie in the dark and think about things. It's then I know what Sparks said was right and then again it's so chuffing philosophically intangible why bother? Why not just get on with things. Get down on the tarmac and let life kick the shit out of you.

– What about Madeleine?

I ask naively but he just shrugs.

– We are told this and we are told fucking that. Why? Why do they keep us down. Who keeps us down? One rule for them, one for us. Why can't we just live and be happy? Too fucking simple that's why.

– Ah ha!

I announce, thinking that I am beginning to catch his drift.

– This is starting to sound like a full blown out of order conspiracy theory Sparksy baby.

I say self congratulatory. He stops and turns and faces me. The cool mid morning breeze ruffles his thick black hair.

– I'm talkin' about freedom Cal, and there sure as Christ ain't no freedom here for us.

– Freedom?

– Money, Lira, filthy lucre. How the fuck are the likes of us strange bastards ever goin' to make any real dosh? You tell me that.

– Dosh? Fuck man there's more to life than dosh.

– Oh you poor sad fucker. Freedom. There's no fuckin' freedom without your trousers jingling with cash, sucker. That's security. That's why the smart birds marry dessicated old rich guys.

Bewildered I trail after the big prick as he makes his way to the all night petrol station for a Mars Bar. How appropriate don't you think, considering that I am now convinced Sparks is wired to the dark side of Eric Cantana's crutch protector.

And then I'm thinking about Dizzy at that very moment. Lucky Dizzy, spaced popping out, banging away at Sasha King in the wedding bed. Trousers at his ankles, her naked legs wrapped around his thighs, the both of them thrusting like rabbits in the shadowy back court of the tenement building. Have you seen the architecture of the wedding bed? Deep angles and upright shadows. Black and grey and heavy iron. Very . . . Gothic.

I didn't know it but that would be the last time I would see Barry Sparks Drysdale for seven years.

We, me and Dizzy, like most people, grew up. I got married at twenty-five, just graduated, to a girl I met one night in a bar in the East End.

I've never met a girl like you before. Seven bottles of Miller Genuine Draft and Edwyn Collins thumping out across the grubby killing floor of a pub called The Tumbling Star, were the precursors to our meeting. I was with Dizzy and Woody. She, Marsha, was with three of her friends, Angie, Freya and Elaine. Eventually, Dizzy, Woody, Angie, Freya, Elaine, Marsha and me are all standing at the bar grinding out rhythm with Edwyn Collins. We even had the barman put the record on over and over again till we all got it right. All of us up together at the bar doing backing vocals to "I've Never Met A Girl Like You Before".

And that was how I met the future Mrs Calvin Milne, standing singing, blitzed, at the bar of the Tumbling Star, not as I had always imagined it would be, hitching up to some weird bitch from the Friday Karma, bobbing heads to Castle Trancelot and China Zones, forever.

Dizzy married too, not to Sasha King who ran off with a mad axe-wielding taxi driver and later returned to set up home with an accountant, but to a girl who was hooked on valium. Diazepam to the medical fraternity. Throughout their married life, six years exactly, Dizzy's wife, Carole-Anne, was in and out of the local

Mental Hospital. She was, in fact, the living incarnation of totally zapped trance.

Hung up on clinical depression, she eventually flung herself from a bridge and into the path of a train. Zzzzplaaaattttttttt! She had been visiting her sister and had just gone off the moonbeam. Crash! Doof! Leaving my poor mate Dizzy to pick up the splintered pieces and look after their five year old daughter.

Of course my ill-fated attempt at monogamy didn't last either. I hired a suit for eighteen months until I'd paid it off at incredible high interest and put myself about in the city as some kind of high-flyer. We bought a flat near the new roundabout and a parade of shops where the baseball caps and tracksuit females hung out to smoke Wackybacky, sniff glue and Acid their souls out into the creature comfortland of oblivion.

I hated it in that cramped pokey little sophisticated cave that was costing us an arm, leg and a buttock. And the car was always breaking down. I told Marsha I had personalised number plates: C for Calvin, 116 ESJ.

– You are one sad fucker.

She told me as I was screwing her and she was always wanting sex. It got boring indoors after a while so we made love in the shadows of the back court we had once known as the wedding bed. Then on the beach as the tide rolled in around us at midnight. And once in a wheatfield in the early hours of the morning. But things became apparent. Transparent.

It got claustrophobic in the flat. She went out to aerobics. I played five-a-side soccer. She went out to her friends. I looked up sad old Dizzy. She had evening classes on Wednesdays. I played snooker with Woody on a Thursday night. She went uptown on a Saturday. I went to the pub and then the football.

One Saturday in March I went with Dizzy and Woody to the soccer. Afterwards we waited in a long queue for a fish supper at Fabrizio's. We then walked, fish suppers cupped carefully in hands, the full two miles from Fabrizio's to The Cherry Lights pub, near the city centre.

While Dizzy sat and brooded, Woody and me chatted to two girls, Rosa and Carla. By nine, small and cute and morose Dizzy had set off to look for a taxi to take him home. Home where his widowed mother babysat his daughter and waited hopefully for his return.

By one of those mysterious freaks, me and Woody were left with the girls. Two on two, cosy. Made courageous by the bottled liquid, chemical mixing with bodily fluids, I agreed to walk Carla, delicious dark-eyed Carla, home.

And we walked, leaving Woody and Rose playing games with their eyes over bottles of Budweiser and Becks. She impressed me with her culture. A veritable A to Z of art. Botticelli, Fouquet, Goya, Masaccio, Pissaro, Velasquez.

– Velasquez? Didn't he play for Spain in the last world cup?

I heard myself laugh.

– No he was an artist. Though you are correct he was Spanish, born Seville 1599, died Madrid 1660. My joke in the face of this torrent of intellect seemed flat. I felt like a total dickhead.

– Oh?

Sounding really ignorant, was all I could say.

It was her turn to laugh now. A little chuckle came from her calm demeanour. Then she stopped and drew near to me, pressed her lips upon mine, her tongue forcing its way into my mouth. She pushed me back gently against a wall and we continued to kiss. Then I felt her hand over my crotch, undoing my fly, fumbling for my penis.

– Wait,

I said.

– I know a place.

It had rained hard that night, though it was dry now, and the back court was muddy and slippy. I led her through the shadows past the grey and black and heavy iron to the far side of the building to the place we had known years before as the wedding bed.

She was already removing her knickers as I was looking about to make sure that nobody was watching. I felt nervous, for some reason, but she was pulling up her skirt to expose the black forest of hair surrounding her vagina.

She sat and from a sitting position, on the damp concrete,

reached up and touched me on the crotch. Her skirt was now up at the level of her bust and I had a massively aching erection. As she lay there rolling her tongue seductively around her lips I unbuckled my trousers and let them glide gracefully, almost serenely, down to my ankles.

– You disappoint me.

She whispered and I frowned.

– You're wearing underpants and I can't get a good look at your dick.

Removing my kegs I climbed on top and started banging away, surprised at how muddy and litter-strewn the ground was. It was strange because I felt no remorse, no guilt.

Covered in mud, I eventually walked half way across the city, west curving south, to where Carla lived. She invited me in for a coffee but I declined. It was two in the morning and I wondered about Marsha. It took me forty-five minutes to walk, at a powerful pace, back to the flat. It had started to rain, heavily. So by the time I got home I was not only knackered, but soaked as well.

I just wanted to crawl into bed and fall fast asleep, but Marsha had other ideas. Her wide sensual mouth went into overdrive, and she started to rant and rave the moment I walked through the door. Then she was throwing things.

– Not that for fucksakes, that was a present from your . . .

I ducked and the china teapot whistled past my ear to crash against the wall.

– Mum.

And it's over. It's all over. What do I care? Two years of marriage flushed silently down the toilet pan. My suit ruined, and I'd just finished paying for it.

I left that night. Walked half way across the city, north to east, to poor, sad, morose Dizzy. He protests at my arrival, it is almost half past four in the morning, but lends me his sofa to sleep on.

Like an idiot, I'd forgotten to take a note of Carla's phone number. So, next evening, regardless, I make my way to the Cherry Lights. hoping to bump into her. And I do. I find her by the bar, with a big bloke in workmen's overalls. I assume it is her brother Mikey. The one she had told me about the night before.

The big guy it seems has been doing her a favour, decorating her flat. While she excuses herself and takes off to the toilet, I casually inform the big guy about her sexual prowess.

– She's a wonderful shag.

I tell him, only to discover that the Gorilla isn't Mikey, or some casual painter and decorator, but her estranged husband Gordon. When he tells me this, with that screwed up manic look on his face, I just sit there totally nonplussed. Totally stunned.

– So . . .

I begin nonchalantly.

– Are you hoping for a reconciliation?

I shrug, a few seconds before the big man explodes.

Then I'm legging it. Down toward the city centre. The big boy, his beergut jerking from side to side, is running after me and I'm wondering how a big fat lad like this can run so fast.

I make my getaway, and spent the rest of the evening with Dizzy as he picks away at his sanity.

– Carole-Anne was, you know, beautiful man.

He says sullenly.

– She was a good mother, you know.

Personally I doubt if Carole-Anne knew she had a daughter she was so spaced out all the time. Then Dizzy's looking toward the ceiling and pouring pills down his throat.

After two days of this miserable existence, I decide that I have to save my sanity. I pack my meagre belongings and head back to the flat to swallow my pride, beg Marsha for to be forgiven and promise her fidelity. All the way back across the city I'm practising my lines. I'm still engrossed in rehearsals as I reach the flat door and unlock it. As I enter I am aware of a hollow echoing sound as I chant my pledge:

– Marsha,

I am whispering to myself as I walk along the hall.

– I promise you darling I will never, but never . . .

I have opened the door to the living room and stand aghast. The room is totally bollock naked. Empty! Only my clothes, not even the carpet, lie in disarray around the room. I move to collect them only to discover that Marsha has shredded them.

It's enough to make a man weep and I did. Lay down and wept like a baby, curled up like a ball, cuddling what was left of my clothes. I fell asleep like this. So tired, so . . .

Tired.
Golden slumbers.
It had somehow, and I've thought about this a lot, gotten away from me. And where had it gone? The world had turned, Saturday into Sunday. Stability to instability. And somehow I . . . I could feel the wind on my face . . .
My hair blown back.
The wind
of change
perhaps

Corridors
Long lonely empty
corridors,
Sterile and devoid
of colour.

Reaching.
Reaching out
for a hand to help
you get back up to where
you were, and you can just feel
the flesh when all at once you've let
go and you find yourself falling backwards towards the darkness.

It's dark when I awake. Light, splintered, casts queer solitary shadows on the unsmiling walls of the flat. I think about my childhood and the sunshine coruscating from the glass of cars. My father walking, striding home from work. My mother sending me out to meet him. Deep unsettling poignancy forces me to banish such joy from my memory.

I stand and stretch and make my way slowly to the door. I go out without looking back. Down the cold concrete steps and out into the street night. I have nowhere to go and don't know where I'm going.

Three years later I'm scraping by. Living in a bedsit in the seediest part of the East End. Selling the Evening Gazette on the station platform. There is a train due in from Manchester so, tonight, I am out there waiting.

Christ, Carla was thrown out of the bar on the station concourse the other day. Exposing herself to the punters, again. Blitzed, completely stoned right out of her mind. I kept my head down as she staggered past calling back toward the pub as she went.

– Fush you, bashtars!

She paused, momentarily, and held me in her glazed gaze, faint recognition in her swaying eyes. Then she cursed and sloped off zig-zagging toward the taxi ramp.

The Manchester train pulled in to the platform. I hovered, bellowing:

– Eeee'nin Gazette!

I saw him step down off the train and my heart missed a hundred beats. He saw me immediately and waved. I wanted to hide. To runaway and hide but he beat a hurried path straight to me.

– You want a paper? Sparks?

He laughed.

– I'll have the fucking lot Calvin you crazy bastard.

I touched the material his suit was made of, like a peasant might once have touched the hem of his Lord's robe.

– Wow, Sparksy baby, where did you get the money to buy a fucking Armani?

– Not to mention the Ralph Lauren tie.

He beamed.

We are in The Angels Overdrive, the most expensive place in the city. The restaurant in the sky. He has bought me my evening meal, and is now watching me eat. He has rented a flat in the city and has asked me to come over the next day, he might have something for me.

– So you're down on you luck?

He asks.

– No, not really, I . . . I . . . just wanted freedom.

– Freedom? Christ Cal, what you've got is chains. You do what everybody else tells you to do. Be there, go here. Chains. What I've got is freedom because . . .

– Because?

I interrupted begging him to tell me the secret.

– Because I've got dosh.

– How?

– How? How? I'll tell you how. The only way strange fuckers like us can ever have freedom.

I frowned and he promised to explain everything to me the next day. He lifted the brandy glass to his lips and his wrist dripped gold.

Strange fuckers and he included himself in that and then again, perhaps, we are all strange.

That night I sat in my bedsit in the dark, the television buzzing away in the background, and sipped at a bottle of Sol. Outside cars whooshed past, and I wondered where they were headed and who was driving them. Strange fuckers, perhaps.

The next morning I met Sparks at Fabrizio's and he bought me a coffee and a bacon roll.

– Christ man, you're in some fucking state. You sleep in those clothes?

– Well I thought I was coming here to meet an old chuffing mate, not to take part in a fashion show.

Sparks laughed, took a drink of his coffee and grimaced.

– Jees! Fabrizio's coffee hasn't changed!

It was my turn to laugh.

He, strange fucker, took me to his car, a brand new Audi, and asked me if I wanted to assist him.

Assist him do what?

– You'll see.

So we both climbed into his car and set off for the outskirts of the city. We drove to the faraway hill, the one that overlooks the city, and parked at the viewpoint parking area near the top. Barry told me to carry a metal box, he had taken out of the boot, and follow him.

– What's in the box?

I asked him casually.

– I'm paying you to carry it, not to ask question.

Paying me? My eyes light up. I am desperate for cash. I am two weeks behind with the rent and I can't afford to lose the roof over my head. I wonder how much he intends to pay me, but don't like to ask. We climb to, almost, the highest vantage point on the hill before Sparks stops and says simply.

– This'll do.

The metal box is getting heavy and my legs are hurting from the climb. I slump down onto the grass, breathing heavily and coughing.

Sparks stood above me, looking back down the way we had come. He had a pair of binoculars in his hand and every now and then he lifted them to his eyes and looked through them.

– What are you looking for?

I asked, but received no answer, he just continued to search the lower reaches of the hill. At length he dropped down beside me and smiled.

– Well, we'll just have to wait.

– For what?

He didn't answer and we did wait. For well over an hour we sat on the grass in the sunshine and talked about the old days. A small wind got up and I had to return to the car for my sweater. I had just reached the car when out of the corner of my eye I saw Sparks suddenly leap to his feet. In no time he had the binoculars to his eyes before turning to the metal box, opening it, and scrabbling about in the box for something.

So I'm pulling on my sweater, pretending nothing is happening, and calling over to him:

– I'm telling you man, Dizzy's totally tranced.

And when I turn he has assembled a semi-automatic weapon from the metal box.

– Get in the car!

Sparks calls out as he raises the rifle to his shoulder. I walk round to the passenger's side but he calls out from the corner of his mouth:

– The driver's side you prick! And have the engine running, ready to blow out of here man!

You don't fuck around with a man who can, obviously, shoot a gun. So I race around to the driver's side and am just ready to climb in when I hear the gun go off, twice. Kapokrak! Kapokrak! I look down the hill. People away in the distance are looking about themselves in panic. Children are running screaming to their mothers and a man sitting on a rug, having a picnic presumably, with a young lady and another couple, has just fallen over dead. The woman, presumably his wife or lover, is screaming, her dress spattered in blood.

Sparks has ran round to the passenger's side and is telling me through gritted teeth:

– Get in the fucking car and drive.

I obey. No choice. I need the money and I don't want blood spurting from a bullet hole in my head, like the picnic man. Nevertheless I find it difficult to believe what I have just witnessed.

We drive back to the city. I put the foot down, but Sparks commands that I slow down.

– Take it easy. We don't want to look like we're escaping from the scene of a crime now do we?

I tell him that what he has just done is immoral.

– Immoral? What the fuck you know about immoral? A quick shag in the wedding bed with some other guy's tarty wife? Life is immoral you dick. There are people out there with millions, multi-millions, and people out there with less than nothing, minus, you know, like negative fucking equity. There are people out there who are so obese they can't even walk, and still others who are so hungry and emaciated they can't walk either. Listen Cal, you self-righteous little prick, the whole world's fucking immoral man, I mean who gives a shit anyway? Nobody that's who.

> Maybe
> He's right.
> Who knows.
> But what is that he is saying?
> On the railtrack of existence, heaven and hell
> are adjacent platforms in the same station.
> Perhaps?

We went back to Sparks' flat. Psychedelic luxury in Yuppiedom. He played me his favourite Depeche Mode, "Never Let Me Down Again". And I watched him pack. I watched him take blown-up monochrome photographs of the man he has killed, a notorious local drug baron a rival consortium had paid Sparks handsomely to dispose of, and tear them up, carefully, into tiny little pieces.

– Tomorrow . . .

He says

– I have to head south. I'll relax for a few days with my girlfriend Gillian, she's a lawyer, then I've got some work to do in Europe.

He gives me his address, and makes me promise to look him up anytime I'm in his adopted city. I nod a reluctant hollow promise. I'll never have the money to visit. I'm trapped in this city. But I don't admit this to Barry.

Then he hands me twenty thousand pounds for assisting him. I flap out. Eyes wide, thanking him, talking like a machine gun going off. Later I calm down and we talk into the early hours and then I walk home across the city to my bedsit, the whole day feeling like a surreal dream of the cartoon variety. The night of this city making me resemble a speck of minute dust in some higher power's living room. Joy!

The next day I go uptown shopping. I buy myself some new gear then call in at the Tumbling Star for a few refreshments. But I sit alone watching people come and go, and my new found happiness coinciding with my new found wealth descends into dire loneliness and brooding depression. What a mess my life has become. When someone plays Edwyn Collins' "I've Never Met A Girl Like You Before", I think "Fuck this" and leave to walk home to my bedsit.

I watch some television, or at least I have it buzzing away in the background as I stare obliquely at the screen.

I am wakened by a persistent rapping at my door. It is seven thirty. I rise groggy, and stagger wearily to the front door, wearing nothing but my boxer shorts. I open the door and two bull-neck gorillas have grabbed me by the shoulders, and are pulling me back inside the flat. They demand three weeks' rent, as they pin me to the floor and punch my face. They call me names.

– Lazy bastard.

– Idle good for nothing wanker.

I reply that I have a degree from the city's top university and the bigger of the two men punches me hard on the side of the head. So hard I see stars, stars and stars.

– Three weeks' rent, prick!

they demand and I am about to pay them out of the twenty thousand Sparks had given me for assisting him, when for some inexplicable reason I threaten them.

– I'll give you three seconds to let me go or . . .

They laugh. As I lie there on the floor, the bigger of the two men takes what's left of the milk in my fridge and pours it all over me. They tell me I have seven days to come up with the money, or . . .

I shower, shave and dress quickly, suddenly taking an interest in my appearance once more, and walk to Fabrizio's, where I breakfast on my new found wealth. Sparks is right, the coffee in here is dreadful. Funny how I never noticed how bad it was before.

I decide I need work, but not just any job, not just any occupation any strange fucker can handle. Not just any job that allows me to be shackled to the yoke of a mortgage and the chains of work, going round and round until the earth stops spinning on its axis and stands still, and you feel as if you are circling your own existence. And then maybe Sparks does need an assistant.

I go back to the bedsit and write the landlord a note. SCREW YOU. Then I catch a taxi to the station and board a train heading south. As the train pulls out of the station the guy selling the Evening Gazette is screaming, "New Labour Landslide Prompts Conservative Leadership Battle!" At the same time I look at the piece of paper in my hand and check Sparks' address. Some anonymous house, in an anonymous street, in an anonymous city.

Freedom. Such a very simple, uncomplicated thing.
Why him and not me? I find myself asking . . . Why has
he got dosh, and freedom, and not me? Now, though, I want
it, and I want it badly.
Because . . .

And then, in my head, I can hear
China Zones and I can see Dizzy, Jerk, jerk, jerk with
with the weird

weird
weird
weird
till all is
all is
dark
oh
so
very
d
a
r
k..

And monday
is vanishing
into blueness.

# Biographies

**Jane Beeson** was born in Surrey but spent part of her childhood in the South West and now lives in Devon. She studied at the Slade, exhibiting at the Arnolfini, Bristol and various London galleries. In 1973, she gave up her career as a painter to go to university, and since then has written for radio, television and stage, as well as publishing four novels. Her most recent novel, *Scarhill*, was published by Heinemann in 1995. Her most recent play, *Carrington*, was produced at the Chichester Minerva Theatre.

Her poetry has won prizes, been read on *Poetry Now*, Radio 3 and on Radio 4, and published in magazines and anthologies. Most recently she has been in the *Phras* '94 and '95 *Open Poetry Winners Anthology* and the *ME Research Winners Anthology*. Her first collection was published by Headland; her second, *Quartz*, will be published by the same publishers in late-1997.

**Tom Bryan** was born in Canada of Irish-Canadian and Scottish parents in 1950, but has long been resident in Scotland. Has published two poetry collections – *Wolfwind* (Chapman, Edinburgh) and *North East Passage* (Scottish Cultural Press, Aberdeen), both in 1996; has also published several short stories and had fiction broadcast on BBC. Editor of *Northwords* 1992–97 and *The Broken Fiddle* 1994–97, and writer-in-residence for Aberdeenshire Council, 1994–97. A non-fiction book about colourful Scots in North America will be published by Thistle Press in late-1997.

**George Walker Burns**, born just outside Edinburgh now lives in Kilmarnock, where his father was a railway signalman and his mother worked in a local cafe. He left school before 16 to work in a carpet factory; made redundant, he entered the University of Glasgow, obtaining an honours degree and, later, postgraduate qualifications at Paisley and Strathclyde. Now works for the local education department. Has had several poems published, and has recently written a screenplay for the London director Ed Braman and Pearl Catlin Associates. Has researched and written documentary proposals for a Guildford-based production company.

**Amanda Dalton** was a deputy head teacher in a Leicester comprehensive school for some years, and now works for the Arvon Foundation at Lumb Bank in Yorkshire. She has had many poems published in magazines, along with two pamphlet collections: *The Dad Baby* (Waldean Press 1995) and *Room of Leaves* (Jackson's Arm, 1996). She was a prize winner in the 1994 and 1996 National Poetry Competitions.

**Jonathan Davidson** was born in 1964 and grew up in Didcot, Oxfordshire. Has worked in the Midlands and the North, and now lives in Coventry. He works as Literature Officer for Birmingham Libraries. His collection of poems, *The Living Room*, was published by Arc Publications in 1994.

**Angela Dove** was born in Leeds in 1951 and moved to London in 1969. Trained as a theatre designer and actress, her main career has been in the professional theatre. Has recently been an information officer with The Poetry Society and is now developing her career as a writer and teacher. Recent work has appeared in anthologies and magazines, including *Poetry Review*.

**John Godfrey**, born in Bristol, has lived in Hitchin for the past nineteen years, and has been writing intermittently since 1988. Reads at the Ware Arts Centre poetry readings and has had poems published in *New Spokes*, *ASWELLas*, *Fatchance* and *Acumen*. His first collection, *Replaying the Echo*, was published by Rockingham Press in 1995.

**John Gohorry** is 54 and lectures in Organisation Theory. His second collection of poems, *Talk Into the Late Evening*, (Peterloo, 1992) was a Poetry Book Society recommendation. He is trying to place a third, and is working towards a first collection of short fiction.

**John Gurney** has been writing full-time since retiring as a senior lecturer on degree courses in 1985. He won first prize in the Bridport Poetry Competition in 1992 and was a supplementary prize-winner in 1995. His most recent publications are *War*, an epic poem of fifteen thousand lines, and a collection of *Three Verse Plays*, both published by the University of Salzburg Press.

**Len Krisak** teaches English Literature at Stonehill College, near Boston. His poems have appeared in such publications as *Orbis*, *Envoi* and *The Dark Horse* in the UK and in *Cumberland Poetry Review*, *The Formalist*, *The Lyric* and *Tennessee Review* in the US. He has won a number of prizes.

**Judith Lal** was born in the north Cotswolds in 1975, of Indian father and English mother. Attended Norwich School of Art and Design, specializing in creative writing in her third year. In her poetry, she aims to combine powerful images of nature with a humane sense of subtle humour.

**Anne Lewis** was born and brought up in Welsh-speaking Wales, and now lives on Anglesey. She trained as as taxonomic zoologist and, after various jobs, now combines a job as part-time administrative assistant with biological/taxonomic illustration.

Under her married name of Anne Alexander, she has illustrated two major Shore Guides for tropical regions; the most recent, *A Guide to the Sea-Shores of Tropical East Africa* is to be published by SAREC in late-1997. Her novels for children have won the Welsh Academy Award (1994) and the Tir Na'n Og Prize (1996).

**Clare MacDonald Shaw** teaches English Literature and MA Writing courses at Nottingham Trent University. Her poems have appeared in various magazines and anthologies, including *London Magazine*, *Poetry Wales*, *The Poetry Book Society Anthology 1992*, *The Arvon International Anthology 1993* and the *TLS Poems on the Underground Competition Booklet* in 1996. A first short collection will be published in autumn, 1997 by Shoestring Press.

**Trevor McMahon** was born in 1951 and lives in Bangor. Has published widely in various magazines, periodicals and anthologies. With William Peskett he founded, edited and published the poetry magazine *Caret* in the 1970s.

**Amanda Metcalfe** is 40 and lives in Richmond, Surrey. After a variety of jobs, she spent six years working as an arts and history researcher for BBC TV. She left the BBC to paint, but began writing instead. Has written a novel and a handful of short stories, and is currently working on a play. All her work is closely autobiographical.

**William Palmer** was born in 1945. His poems and short stories have been widely published and broadcast. His fourth novel, *The Pardon of Saint Anne*, was published by Jonathan Cape in 1997.

**Sheenagh Pugh**, born in 1950, lives in Cardiff, where she works as a freelance writer and part-time tutor at the University of Glamorgan. Her prize-winning poem 'Crossing the Bridge' was suggested by an incident in a book of eighteenth-century diaries in her local library, Canton, Cardiff. The library was later torched by a vandal and the book destroyed, with many others. She has had eight collections published, including *Id's Hospit* (Seren Books, 1997).

**Philip Raines** lives and works in Glasgow. He is a member of the Glasgow Science Fiction Writers Circle and has contributed to their anthology *Shipbuilding: New SF from Scotland.* His fiction is usually written in collaboration with Harvey Welles; *Fado* is his first solo story.

**Ciarán Ruby** was born in Cork of Irish-Australian parents. After studying and working in England, returned to Cork where she now lives, writing and playing traditional Irish music. Currently a member of the Cork Women's Poetry Circle writing group.

**Suhayl Saadi** was born in 1961 and lives in Paisley, Scotland. Short-listed for University of Glasgow/Radio Clyde Prize for short story, *A Night on the Town,* in 1990, and his short story, *Magpies,* was published in *Inkshed* magazine in 1991. His novel, *The Snake,* is to be published by Creation Books in late-1997. Two other novels are currently with publishers for consideration.

**Penny Simpson** worked as a journalist, theatre reviewer and lecturer after graduating from Brighton Art College and Essex University. She is a former TMA Theatre Critic of the Year, and has received a bursary from the Arts Council of Wales to write her first novel. She has contributed to an anthology of short stories to be published by Bloomsbury in October, 1997.

**Alex Smith** is 53 and lives in Saffron Walden. After thirty years in the City, he now works in the Civil Service. His main interests are English literature, jazz and classical music, history and economics. His poetry is heavily influenced by the landscape of East Anglia, and also of Cornwall. His first collection, *The Appetites of Morning, The Languor of Afternoons,* was published by the University of Salzburg Press in 1996.

**Alison Spritzler-Rose** has published two books: a limited edition with Clarion Press (featuring 'Cows', which was a winner in the 1995 Bridport Prize), and a collection which co-won the 1996 Staple Prize. She was fifth in the 1997 Peterloo Competition. Her work has appeared in the *Observer* and *The Printer's Devil.* She writes a regular column for The Erotic Print Society Review.

**Alan Tuppen** is 52; he was born and brought up in the Midlands, but has lived in London ever since, apart from four years in the Far East in the 1970s. At present he works in a garden centre. Was a finalist in the 1995 London Writers Competition run by the London Arts Board with his story *Lost and Found,* which was published in the winners' collection by Serpent's Tail.

**Joan Wiles** began writing for the theatre in 1991 when she joined STAGEWrite, Salisbury Playhouse Writers' Group. Her first play, *Voyage in the Dark*, an adaptation of the novel by Jean Rhys, ran for four weeks on the London fringe in 1992, and had a second production at the Young Vic in 1996 before touring nationally with the Sphinx Theatre Company. Her poems and reviews have appeared in various magazines. She has taught creative writing for the past nine years.